THE SURVIVOR

Other Books by Robb White

For Young People

CANDY
DEEP DANGER
FLIGHT DECK
THE HAUNTED HOUND
THE LION'S PAW
MIDSHIPMAN LEE
MIDSHIPMAN LEE OF THE NAVAL ACADEMY
THE NUB
SAIL AWAY
SAILOR IN THE SUN
SECRET SEA
THE SMUGGLER'S SLOOP
THREE AGAINST THE SEA
TORPEDO RUN
UP PERISCOPE

Non-Fiction

IN PRIVATEER'S BAY
OUR VIRGIN ISLAND

Novel

RUN MASKED

THE SURVIVOR

by Robb White

Doubleday & Company, Inc.
Garden City, New York

Library of Congress Catalog Card Number 64–16238
Copyright © 1964 by Robb White
All Rights Reserved
Printed in the United States of America

This book is dedicated to
Ben Masselink
and
my brother
John White
Two legendary members of the Marine Corps

THE SURVIVOR

BOOK ONE
Nightmare

1 The man, wounded to the point of death, was awakened by a sound. The sound, being different and closer than the other sounds around him, struck through to the mechanism of his brain, as yet unwounded, and woke him up.

He found that he was slumped, half sitting, with his back against some metal object. His bare and bloody legs and feet stretched out awkwardly down what appeared to be a narrow corridor. Blood was pouring from some wound in his body and there were flies around him.

There was light coming from somewhere, but the place was fairly dark and cool.

Perhaps, he thought, he was in some sort of church, for there were pews, thickly padded, on each side of the aisle in which he sprawled.

There was a window and through it he could see the tops of green palm trees, the fronds waving to him in the wind.

He was in a church. Or, perhaps, lying in the aisle of an airplane.

An odd thought, as complete as a little cloud drifting in an empty sky, floated into, and across and out of his mind. He thought: I am the only American left alive on this island. Something has happened to all the rest and I am the only one alive. Then he thought: Perhaps I am the only American left alive anywhere in the world. If this is true, he thought, then I am the only person who knows what it feels like to be an American. The only person who knows *how* to be an American.

Then he said to himself, "I'd better not die. Not because I'm important but because what I know is important. No, I'd better not die."

Then that thought drifted away and he wondered again what had waked him up. There was music coming from somewhere but that had not waked him. It seemed to him that it had been a voice. A voice close to him and, now as he remembered it, full of menace.

The man looked then at the details of his situation. He was hurt, for blood was coming out of him and the flies were buzzing around, lighting and flying again. Purposeless, they seemed. But there had been purpose in the voice which had awakened him; purpose and threat.

There were some shoes near him. Shoes with high uppers; shoes such as they wore in Texas and the Air Corps—boots almost.

White trousers were above the shoes and above the trousers was a white jacket with a pretty red sash across it.

The man raised his head a little higher.

The enemy was standing there looking down at him, a pistol in his hand.

To the man the enemy looked small and—mean. He would have preferred an enemy of great height and strength and,

even with the gift of death, dignity. Not this little meanness
like a bad-tempered little feisty dog.

It was not, really, the enemy in his white uniform and
pretty sash.

It was the pistol.

Even the pistol was of no stature and it was shoddily
made and badly put together, the parts of it not fitting properly, the trigger guard screwed on and the screw slots
burred by carelessness. There were even rusty spots on the
enemy's pistol and the man doubted if the action worked
with the creamy smoothness of a United States marine's gun.

It was not good, the man thought. The enemy was small
and mean and his pistol was mean and rusty and, the marines
said, made a disagreeable angry little yelp when it fired.
It had none of the power and authority of a Colt .45, none
of that arm-jarring slam of the .45.

But it could kill you, this little gun. And it was going to
kill him.

The man remembered now what had awakened him. It
had been the enemy saying, in English, "American, you die."

The man could do nothing. His wounds held him with simple weakness against the seat, all his strength having drained
out of him. He could not raise his hand, nor draw up his legs
to rise from the floor. It took all his strength just to raise
his head high enough so that he could look beyond the pistol
to the face of the enemy.

Above the immediate silence between him and the enemy
the man heard a band playing, a diesel motor running somewhere, even the far pounding of the surf against the coral
reef. But no voices.

The man was now sad for he had, finally, failed. He and
the marines.

They had come so far and endured so much only, now, to
fail. It made him sad, and to feel his life flowing away and

to see the pistol which would put a final end to it made him feel, as he had felt before, that he was a failure. Somehow, he thought, everything I try to do fails. The things he knew: the details of the enemy, the numbers of him here, the guns and planes and facilities he had would, because he was dying and the marines were dead, never be known to those who desired and needed to know. And because they would not now know the strength of the enemy their attack on this place would be murderously expensive.

That made him sad and the manner now of his dying made him sad. He hated lying helpless here.

It was not right.

The man looked up at his enemy and said, in the enemy's own oddly soft and singsong language; said it aloud and with authority. "I will not die in this contemptible fashion."

The explosion was so close to his head that it added a small, sharp pain to all his pain.

Then a slow darkness moved toward him, covered him, pressed him completely down into his own blood on the floor.

The man did not die immediately. Instead, he seemed to drift backward down the flow of his life.

He could not remember now how he came to be on this island nor how long he had been here, but he did remember that it had been a long and painful time. A time of endless fear, day and night; a time of being hunted and having the feeling of a thing that is being hunted and has no escape from, nor any defense against, his hunters.

There had been others with him, the marines, but they were not with him now and he did not know where they were but suspected that they, too, had been finally hunted down by this enemy and killed.

There had been a purpose for his coming here but this purpose was draining away with his blood into the carpet of the airplane. The purpose was lost; everything was lost.

The man felt strongly that he did not want to die. Not yet, at any rate. It was not, he thought, *time* for him to die.

The man, all strength gone, enclosed in darkness and pain, could do nothing. He lay there, dying, almost naked, his body torn with wounds and scars and cuts, his beard ragged and unshaven, his feet bare. . . .

The dying man's name was Adam Land, twenty years old, a naval aviator with the rank of lieutenant (junior grade), U. S. Naval Reserve.

The place where he lay dying was Enulab Island in the Micronesian group of islands scattered like tiny, but lethal dots in the vastness of the Central Pacific Ocean.

The time of his dying was 1943.

This book is the story of how Lieutenant (j.g.) Adam Land, USNR, came to Enulab Island. The events in this book, the people, the boats and ships and the islands are not real, but the war was real and, in the desperate days after the sneak attack on Pearl Harbor, the need for such ventures as this was real and, in fact, such ventures were carried out.

In the months after Pearl Harbor, with the United States Navy crippled and almost ruined, nothing could prevent the enemy from spreading an enormous spiderweb across the Pacific toward the shore of America. With fleets of ships and armies of men he overran millions of miles of ocean and land, establishing on the more choice islands bases from which he could continue his outward sweep and, also, protect what he had stolen. With his ships and planes operating from these outer islands he ruled the Pacific from Alaska to Australia's Barrier Reef and denied it to the U. S. Navy.

The situation was intolerable, but it took the lives of thousands of men and many ships to cure it.

Adam Land was one of the men thrust out into the Pacific against the enemy waiting there.

2 Adam Land's plane was fifth in the landing pattern and that grabbed him. Four of the old Douglas Dauntless SBDs were flopping around in front of him, wasting his time, wasting the whole afternoon, wasting the tide and the surf. How could any airplane go so *slow?*

His own SBD chugged along, waiting, while the green and brown and patterned fields of Oahu slid like something on a slow conveyor belt below him. Off to his left he could see the ocean, to his right the cloudy mountains and the long gray road twisting toward Honolulu.

"Come on! Come *on!*" Adam said aloud, urging the planes ahead of him to get on with it; get down on the ground, get out of his way. He debated for a moment opening the throttle and blasting in under the four planes ahead of him. He could tell the operations officer that it was an emergency. But then he reflected that he was in a good deal of trouble already—missed flights, late to the line, failure to relieve. He had better, he decided, watch his step for a little while or they'd confine him to the base and he'd miss all that surf.

The surf out here in the Hawaiian Islands was *terrific.* It made the surf he had known along the coast of California look like beginners' waves. Out here they came in, great blue humped-back *monsters,* and when they hit these coral reefs surged up ten, twenty, thirty feet high. With their tops now in the wind and the spray blowing they came on, some for a mile or more, with their slopes smooth and fast, giving you a ride like nothing else in the world.

Then when they curled and broke they made a tube of

water as smooth and perfectly formed as blue steel. A tube so big that all you had to do was crouch down on the board and race through it, the water all around you, completely, but not touching you. Then you broke out of the tunnel, rammed the board up and over and headed back for the sea again as, behind you, the wave broke on the shore with a crash that shook the land and tore chunks and pieces out of it.

Wild, man.

Yesterday, a marine from La Jolla, surfing with Adam had never come out of a tunnel. Adam thought about him now, for a moment. These waves weren't for beginners and they weren't for these California tigers who had no respect for them. They were man-killers with no regard for who you might think you were.

Adam looked over at the surf breaking near the Marine Base at Ewa and even from his altitude he could see that the waves were running high and breaking close to the shore. It would be a little dangerous this afternoon (if he *ever* got down out of this airplane) and he decided to take charge of the girl Gloria. She wasn't, he thought, really a tiger, she just wanted to make you think she was so she'd take a wave when it was too big and fast and breaking too short. With this surf she'd better not do that, he decided. Or she'd get her pretty self slaughtered.

Just thinking about the girl and the surf and the lonely beach, and then the soft Hawaiian night, made him more impatient with the planes still ahead of him.

"Come on! Come *on!*" he yelled into the wind. "Don't take all day."

And, finally, the sky was empty ahead of him and he slapped the SBD down on the runway, braked it up hard and short, slammed it around to the taxi strip and then, the wheels almost floating, taxied it in toward the hangar. As he climbed out, now in a real hurry, the squadron operations officer stopped him.

"You've got a great future as a taxi driver, Adam, but not much as a pilot."

Adam had never liked the operations officer much. He was a good deal older than most of the people in the squadron; a ground officer who spent his time criticizing the way you flew the airplane.

"I'll do until you get your wings," Adam told him and started over to check in his chute.

"The C.O. wants to see you. Right away," the op officer said.

Adam turned around. "What for?"

"For being such a dashing aviator, I guess."

"Come on! Is this a gag?"

"How should I know. I have here a message which states in plain English: 'Have Lieutenant Adam Land report to the commanding officer immediately.'"

"Look, ol' buddy," Adam said, "do me this great favor, will you? Just don't see me. I came in way down the strip and parked in the Baker Area and when you got there with your message I had gone. Vanished. Disappeared. Do that for me like a good buddy."

"Ol' buddy," the operations officer said, "I'd do anything for you except get mine in a sling. I've delivered the message. You can do anything you want to about it. It's a free country, you know."

"Friendship," Adam said angrily, slamming his chute pack down on the counter. "Land!" he yelled at the enlisted man behind it. "A as in AWOL. One lousy parachute."

"A. Land," the sailor said, writing in a notebook. "I'll pass on your opinion to the parachute riggers, sir."

Adam ignored him and then, in the sunshine again, stopped for a moment and listened to the surf, a faint, dis-

tant sound. It made him think of the guys in California—
the surfers. Nothing—food, drink, money, job—*nothing* could
keep the surfers away from the surf. All day, every day they
would be on the beaches. They would start before dawn, the
long surfboards sticking out of whatever kind of old heap
they could find and make run and head for the surf. And
there they would stay until night fell; and some would stay
through the cold nights, sitting around beach fires, the long
boards waxed and stacked, waiting for the morning surf. The
waves were their life and nothing else mattered to them;
nothing else was important. They were Robin Hoods, steal-
ing from the rich in the grand houses along the Malibu
Beach to give to the poor surfers squatting around the little
fires. Nothing could stop those tigers from going to the waves
—not the fierce cold winds, nor rain, nor hunger, nor police.
Nothing—

The squadron C.O. was a good joe, Adam thought, and
whatever he wanted now couldn't be so important that it
couldn't wait a little while. If it was a big hot thing like
shipping out to Guadalcanal or some place where there was
some fighting going on the C.O. would want to see all hands,
not just him.

The last time he'd gotten a "report to the C.O." all the
commander had wanted was for him to check his flight log.
Probably that was all he wanted now. Some little thing that
could wait until tomorrow. You just couldn't waste a time
like this with the sun shining and the surf coming in like
cream and a girl like Gloria waiting for him. Even in war
you needed rest and relaxation; it said so in the book. . . .

In the squadron office the C.O. and the exec were talking
about Adam Land. "Land in trouble again?" the exec asked.

The C.O. picked up a message slip and looked at it. "Must
be. And this time we can't help him, Charlie." The C.O. slid
a slip of paper across the desk to the exec.

The exec read it and whistled softly through his teeth.

The C.O. took the paper back and locked it in the wall safe. "Those orders came straight to me. They didn't even go through the group commander, Charlie."

"I wonder what he's done now?" the exec asked. "What *can* a guy do to rate top-secret orders confining him to his quarters?"

"That's what worries me," the C.O. said. "This is no little thing. It's not even an ordinary general court-martial thing —that wouldn't have to be secret, even if it was a moral turpitude charge. Whatever Land has done, it's very big and very serious."

"I'm no admirer of Land, as you are, Skipper," the exec said, "but still I can't see him involved in anything big. Breaking curfew, okay, or going to some beach that's out of bounds, or missing flights. But nothing big enough to rate that." He pointed to the locked safe. "Land's still wet behind the ears."

"I wish there was something I could do to help the kid—" the C.O. said, looking out the window.

"You read the last sentence, didn't you?" the exec said. "'These orders are not to be questioned nor discussed.'"

"That's why I can't help him," the C.O. said.

"I wouldn't miss Land much if this thing got him clean out of the squadron," the exec said.

"I would," the skipper said.

"So he can fly a plane real fine. At Pensacola and San Diego and here. But nobody's shot at him."

"Nobody's shot at any of 'em," the skipper said. "Except you and me."

"Well, I don't know," the exec said. "Land's attitude is what grabs me."

"So he's a playboy . . . on the ground. But he flies the

NIGHTMARE   *11*

airplane and hits the target better than most of them. That's
what counts."

"If a guy doesn't *care*—and our boy Land doesn't even
know there's a war on—what's going to keep him around
when things get rough?"

The C.O. looked at the exec and was worried. "Don't you
think he'll stick around?"

"Look," the exec said, "I don't know what anybody'll do
when the sky starts filling up with those AA bursts and
you've got ten Zeroes on your tail. But it just seems to me
that the rest of the pilots are interested in getting on with
the war. That sort of thing. All Land is interested in is sliding around in the surf on a greasy plank and showing off to the wahines."

The C.O. thought about that for a while, and it bothered
him, but then he said, "Charlie, I know you've got to have all
this stuff on the ground—discipline and training and all that.
But to me the important thing is up in the airplane. Deliver
what they tell you to deliver and if something gets in your
way, knock it down. What difference does it make what
Land thinks about—or doesn't think about—as long as he de-
livers what they give him to deliver?"

"Okay," the exec said, "but when I had to deliver something it seems to me that it took all my little brain could
manage just to do that. There wasn't any room in it for girls
and surfboards and the shape of waves."

The C.O. studied the exec's face for a while, trying to see
all the way into his mind. Finally he asked quietly, "Are you
trying to tell me that Land is a coward, Charlie?"

"A coward? Who knows? Maybe we're all cowards. But
Land is such a *kid!*"

"Aw, Charlie, they're all kids," the C.O. said and looked
out the window at the squadron pilots walking toward the
ready room. "That's the trouble with a war," he said, talking

to himself. "It takes all the young kids and expects them to be men *right now*." He turned back to the exec. "That's the only trouble with Land—if it's a trouble. He just doesn't pretend to be a man as hard as the rest of 'em."

"Well, I think this is what they call an academic discussion," the exec said. "I think this squadron has seen the last of Adam Land."

They both turned to look at the door as someone knocked. Then the C.O. said quietly, "No discussion of this thing, Charlie. I'm going to give him the word and that's all—come in!"

Adam Land, still in the nylon flight suit, came in, closed the door and stood at a careless attention.

The C.O. looked up at him and had a quick, disconnected thought. Adam would make a good model for a recruiting poster saying THE NAVY NEEDS YOU. He was tall and rugged, with brown hair bleached almost gold by all that sitting around on the beach he did. He had a good face, too. Not handsome, hardly even good looking—just a good, simple face, untroubled, a little amused. Happy.

Land's blue eyes bothered the C.O. a little. They were so deep blue and clear and warm and very, very young. There was no trace of concern in them. They seemed to look out upon a world totally without fears or agonies, trouble or—war.

"You want to see me, Skipper?" Adam asked.

"At ease," the skipper said. Suddenly he dreaded giving Land the message and, for a moment, understood how really hard it must be for parents to deny their children something which the child really wanted. "How was the flight?" he asked, putting the thing off.

"Like a bird. What's on your mind, Skipper?"

The exec said, trying to keep the sourness out of his voice, "You got a date or something?"

"You know it. This one's got every brick in the right place."

Such a happy kid, the C.O. thought, with your blue eyes shining in anticipation. And I'm going to let you have it, right between those blue eyes. "Adam," the C.O. said, "you're confined to your quarters until further notice."

The C.O. watched him as, for a second, he didn't even understand the words. Then, when he did, it was as though he had been hit by a poleax—right between the eyes. "What?" Adam asked in a low, unbelieving voice. Then as he really began to understand it he cried, "Oh, no! That can't be, Skipper. I've got a date with the prettiest girl in Hawaii and the surf's perfect."

"You're confined to your quarters, Adam."

"Skipper, there must be a mistake! I haven't done anything. Lately. Not in the squadron. Nowhere!"

"I'm not going to discuss it, Adam. Report to your quarters and stay there."

"But I haven't *done* anything, Skipper. Honest! Nothing! I don't rate this."

But the C.O. only looked at him and he knew there was nothing more.

"What have I done?" Adam said in a weak, almost childish voice, as he turned and walked slowly out.

"Adam!" the C.O. called as Adam was closing the door.

"Yes, sir?"

"You are not to discuss this with anyone either."

"Aye, aye, sir," Adam said listlessly and closed the door.

For a moment the exec and the C.O. sat there looking at the closed door.

"You see," the exec said. "He's a kid."

The C.O. sat for a while looking out the window and then he swung around to his desk, all business. "We'll need a replacement pilot, Charlie. I've got a feeling Land is out of the squadron."

"Okay. I'll go over to ComAirPac this afternoon and see what they've got in the pool."

"Charlie," the C.O. said, "try to find one who can fly an airplane the way Land could. Even if he's just a—kid."

3   Out in the bright sunshine Adam Land was angry at himself. Here he was, almost twenty-one years old and behaving like a kid. He was so close to having tears in his eyes he walked along with his head down so people wouldn't notice. Grow up! he told himself. Or you'll be crying like a baby right here in the middle of the squadron area. Grow up!

"Greetings, Adam," a voice said beside him.

Adam raised his head only high enough to see the leather name tag on the guy's flight suit. "Hi, pal," he said, clearing his throat.

"Going ashore?"

"No."

The man beside him stopped walking for a moment and said in a voice of exaggerated surprise, "The great lover not going ashore! What can this mean?"

"Cut it out," Adam said.

The man fell in step again. "What's eating you?"

"Nothing."

"What'd the skipper want?"

"To pin a medal on me."

"Good-looking medal," the guy said, looking at Adam's chest. "Real good-looking. E Pluribus Wahine. What's the matter? Did oo break oo lil surfboard, Adam?"

"You got real good-looking teeth," Adam said, "but they wouldn't look good where I'm about to push 'em."

"Man, you're in trouble," the guy said.

Adam stopped and looked at him. "What do you mean?"

"Wait! Hold hard! Take it easy, pal!" the guy said, backing away from Adam.

"What do you know about my troubles?" Adam asked.

"Nothing, good buddy. Nothing."

"You said, I was in trouble."

"I mean, just the way you're acting. You look kind of down, that's all. Shook. If you got trouble I don't know anything about it."

Adam started walking again, his hands shoved down in the deep pockets of the flight suit. "No trouble," he said. "No trouble at all."

4 Adam Land was in bachelor officer's quarters talking on the phone to the girl, Gloria, when the marine corps jeep drove up and stopped outside.

"Listen, honey, I *told* you! I can't get out there today . . . Why? Because they're going to pin a medal on me for heroism, is why . . . But tomorrow I'll be there . . . Well, maybe not tomorrow. . . ."

As he went on talking the driver of the jeep, a sergeant in the Marine Corps, came into BOQ and asked at the desk where he could find Lieutenant (j.g.) Adam Land and the man at the desk pointed at the phone booth. The sergeant, a .45 automatic in a holster strapped to his leg, walked over to the phone booth and rapped on the glass door. Adam, still talking to Gloria, turned and looked at him with irritation. The sergeant ignored this and rapped again.

Adam opened the door a crack and said, "Go away, Sergeant. I am talking to a girl. You know, one of those pretty things." Then he closed the door. The sergeant pulled it open and said, "I have orders for you, Lieutenant."

"Listen, honey," Adam said to Gloria, "I'll call you right back, hear? I've got to go win the war now." Then he hung up and glared at the sergeant. "You interrupted me in a conversation vital to the war effort, Sergeant."

The sergeant looked at him with the way sergeants have —not exactly insulting, nor even personal. It's as though you, as a person, don't exist. You're just a unit in the sergeant's mind.

"The jeep's outside, Lieutenant," the sergeant said.

5–6   This marine sergeant is, Adam Land thought:
(a) tongue-tied,
(b) too dumb to talk (but he sure didn't *look* dumb)
(c) just not very talkative.

"Where'd you say we were going, Sergeant?" Adam asked innocently.

"I didn't, Lieutenant," the sergeant said, keeping his eyes on the main road to Pearl Harbor.

"Do you *know* where we're going, Sergeant?"

"I do, Lieutenant."

"Then would you mind very much telling me, since I'm going to find out anyway when we get there?"

"Then you'll know, Lieutenant."

"And how long are we going to stay there, Sergeant? I don't ask this idly but only because I've got a date at Makaha and the tide's turning."

"Long enough, Lieutenant," the sergeant said, stopping the jeep at the Pearl Harbor gate where the marine sentry looked in, read a slip of paper the sergeant held up, saluted, and let them pass.

As they drove along the harbor front Adam was pleased to see that almost all the damage done by the enemy attack had been cleaned up. The first time he'd seen Pearl it had made him sad, and sick, and angry. The ships were still out there in the water, mangled and ruined, Ford Island was still a mess with hangars burned out and skeletons of planes pushed into a somehow shameful heap.

The sergeant stopped the jeep in the marine area and waited until Adam got out, then led him into one of the camouflaged buildings. To another sergeant at a desk the first sergeant said, "This is the lieutenant, Smitty. When you get through with him let me know."

"Wilco. Come on, Lieutenant."

"Whither away?" Adam asked.

"In here," the sergeant said, and opened the door to a small bare room. As Adam came in, the sergeant stood at the door. "Take off all your clothes, everything except your dog tags. Put your gear in that box, tie it up, seal it, put your name and duty station and serial number on it and turn it in to me, sir."

"Look," Adam said, wondering if he was being pushed around. "I'm wearing about everything I own, including two weeks' pay."

"It will all be locked up by the supply officer and returned to you . . . if the occasion warrants. Otherwise it will be sent, intact, to your next of kin."

"Come on!" Adam said, "Fun's fun, but let's don't get carried away. What's all this about?"

"Orders from headquarters, sir. Just strip down." The sergeant looked him over. "Six two, one-sixty, forty-six, twenty-eight, thirty-four, size ten D. Right?"

"You're very good, Sergeant, but I think I'll just go back to my tailor."

The sergeant said ominously, "I wouldn't keep them waiting, Lieutenant," and started for the door.

"Make that in lightweight gabardine, Sergeant, with a little break at the cuffs."

The sergeant looked at him bleakly and closed the door.
He was back in less than two minutes with a laundry bag
which he dumped on the floor, saying, "Here's your outfit,
Lieutenant."

Adam opened the strings of the bag and shook its con-
tents out. There was a suit of marine fatigues, the blouse and
trousers, now stiff with newness and still folded, the dirty-
looking green cloth still a little shiny. There were two pairs
of underpants dyed the same dirty green, and two green
skivvy shirts. There were two pairs of the blotchy green
socks and one pair of the heavy marine boots they called
"boon-dockers." There was one green web belt with the
brass buckle blackened with something. And, worst of all,
a pair of stiff, flat canvas leggings.

And, of course, the two pairs of skivvy tie-ties, also dyed
green.

Since he had nothing else to put on, he got dressed in this
ridiculous outfit, not knowing that he had the leggings on
backward and, although the things fitted him very well, he
felt like that Tin Man in *The Wizard of Oz*. The fatigues
were so new and so starched that they crackled when he
walked and stood out from him in stiff creases.

Gloria was certainly going to be surprised when he appeared in this cockeyed uniform. But, as he looked down
at the two-piece fatigues with the big pockets starched flat
against the cloth he decided that he now looked like a man
of mystery off on a dangerous mission. He could tell Gloria
a real sea story about how all this came about.

The silent sergeant was waiting for him in the hall. "I like
the uniform," Adam said, "but I don't think I'll join up."

The sergeant handed him a long slim piece of stiff cardboard, a short black brush and a bottle of black ink. Adam
saw now that his name "A. Land" had been punched out

of the cardboard. "Stencil that on the back of your jacket," the sergeant said.

"I prefer the gold one with the wings and my rank," Adam said.

"They don't," the sergeant said, motioning him toward the jeep.

Adam got in again, his stiff clothes crackling, and the sergeant drove him to another building where they got out and, again, went up to a desk occupied by another sergeant. "This is the lieutenant," Adam's sergeant said. "I'll wait."

"Ah, the lieutenant," the other sergeant said. "Right this way, Lieutenant."

The sergeant led him into a huge, somewhat dim and cavernous room that smelled of moth balls, oiled leather, grease and mildew. A low, wide counter ran the length of the room and behind the counter were rows of shelves such as those in a library, row after row, with, dimly in the back of the room, bins and boxes. The sergeant leapt neatly over the counter, did an about face and produced a long narrow slip of paper with a list of printed entries on it. "Let's see now," the sergeant said, checking the list. Then he frowned. "Be easier with the field kit full," he said and disappeared into the gloomy rows of shelves. In a moment he reappeared, banged two empty canteens down on the counter and, as he disappeared again, said, "Canteens, two, with stopper."

He came back in a moment with two stiff, folded hunks of canvas and dropped them on the counter. "Canteen covers, two, canvas, with belt hooks."

As the sergeant moved away again Adam picked up a piece of canvas and, with some effort, got it unfolded and read the black letters USMC stenciled on it. The thing was much too small to fit around a canteen, he decided.

The sergeant came back with a three-inch-wide canvas belt, stiff as a board and dotted with brass grommets into some of which black metal hooks had been forced. "Cartridge belt, one, with grommets and hooks. *Right.*"

"I've already got a belt," Adam said, raising the stiff blouse to show him. He pushed the other belt toward the sergeant.

The sergeant seemed offended. "Lieutenant, sir, I have here a list of items to be issued to you. It is not part of my duty to know what you will do with them, or why you need them. But, being government property, it is your duty to take care of them and it is your duty to return them to me when you finish with them. The only excuses I can accept for not returning them are: you get yourself killed, or you get yourself wounded, or you are reported missing—in action, that is, not AWOL—or you are reported a prisoner of war. Sometimes I'll also let guys get away with it if their ship gets sunk. But only by the enemy. Other excuses—and I've heard 'em all, sir—will not do." He disappeared again, to return with two brown bottles. "Halazone, one bottle of twenty-four tablets."

"I know all about your best friend won't tell you," Adam said, "but what's this Halazone for? B.O., or something?"

"The government is not interested in your personal problems, sir," the sergeant said. "But it is interested in keeping you alive so you can fight. Halazone is for purifying water."

"Oh," Adam said.

"Atabrine, one bottle, twenty-four tablets," the sergeant said, putting the other bottle on the counter.

Adam knew about atabrine. "So now you've got me fixed up for pure water and no malaria. But what does the government give me for, say, a bullet hole?"

"That's not my responsibility," the sergeant said. "That's the responsibility of the Medical Department." He went back into the stacks and turned up with his hands full of more of the stiff, folded canvas. He dumped this on the counter and checked his list. "Ammo pouches, six . . . No, no," he said, taking two of them back. "Officers only get four. Enlisted men get six. Ammo pouches, four. Sheath knife, one," he added, tapping one of the canvas objects. "Meat-can cover, one."

Adam waited as the sergeant disappeared again. The counter was littered now with the strange little objects and as he looked at them his amusement began to die. This was taking the whole afternoon.

"Canteen cups, with handle, two," the sergeant said, clanking them down on the counter. "Meat can, with knife, fork, spoon, one." And he clanked that down. "Grease, black, one."

"*What?*" Adam asked, looking at the little packet about the size of a cake of soap.

"For the face and hands, sir. Camouflage. Man of distinction."

Adam had to laugh as he picked up the black grease and looked at it. That was one good thing about the Marine Corps—a surprise a minute.

The sergeant came back with the wickedest-looking dagger Adam had ever seen. The hilt was slim and checkered all over, there was practically no guard, the hilt going directly into a blade in the shape of a long tapered pyramid, sharp on all edges and with a dagger point. The knife was thickly coated with a pale brown grease.

"Good tool," the sergeant said, "particularly for the throat and ribs. Lot better than those old butcher knives the Navy gave us. It would take you five minutes to get one of those into a fellow."

"This is quicker?" Adam asked, looking at the greasy dagger.

"Oh, yeah. And comes out fast, too. Lets you get on with your work."

"Absolutely," Adam agreed, eyeing the dagger.

"Not good for much else, though," the sergeant said, "so I've given you the navy sheath knife, too."

"I've always wanted to be a two-knife type," Adam told him. "Any switch-blades?"

"For kids," the sergeant said. "We don't issue them. Now, if you'll pardon the expression, sir—being an officer you don't get a real gun. You get a little peashooter."

"Don't bother," Adam told him. "I've got a real gun. Lots of 'em. Big ones. Fifty-caliber."

"Ah, so," the sergeant said, disappearing. He came back carrying one of the short-barreled .30-caliber carbines still wrapped in grease with this, in turn, wrapped in brown paper. The sergeant stripped the paper away in one section, rubbed the grease clear and pointed. "Serial number," he said, writing on the slip of paper. "This one, with this serial number, is the only one you can bring back, Lieutenant. You can't just pick up one off the ground and bring that back because, you see, you do that and you foul up some other guy and so he gets himself a gun and so on until finally the whole Marine Corps is fouled up."

"What are we waiting for?" Adam asked.

"Ammo, eight clips, sir." He dropped them on the counter and stood a moment, checking his list. "Oh, yes. Helmet."

"Come *on!*" Adam objected. "No helmet. How can I get the earphones on wearing a tin bucket?"

The sergeant looked worried about this and checked his list again. Then he smiled contentedly. "Look there, Lieutenant. Right there, line eighteen. You see, it says: 'Helmet, combat, with liner and netting—one.'"

"Forget it," Adam told him but the sergeant was already on his way back with a helmet which he put on Adam's head. The liner had not been tied so the helmet plunged down over his eyes and the steel dome of it clanked down on his skull.

This was too much, entirely. Adam wrestled the helmet off and dropped it, clanging, down on the counter. "Look, Sergeant," he said, "let's you and I forget the Marine Corps for a moment and act like two human beings. Okay?"

The sergeant looked as though he had just seen a ghost. "In the Marine Corps, sir, there are no human beings, only marines."

"I know, I know," Adam said. "But just you and I can pretend for a moment. Now, I don't want all this gear. I don't need it. I can't use it. There isn't room in the airplane for it. So, you take it all back." Adam pushed the heap of stuff across the counter toward the sergeant.

At last this sergeant did look like a human being. He pushed the stuff gently back toward Adam. "Keep it, Lieutenant. You may need it. Where you're going."

This was interesting. "Where am I going?"

"You don't know?"

"No, I don't know."

"Neither do I," the sergeant said, "but this is combat gear, so you draw your own conclusions. So—good luck." The sergeant walked away but turned and added, "I hope you bring it back."

"Thanks a lot," Adam said, gathering up the pieces, the dagger and the gun oozing grease all over him, the helmet, back on his head, obstructing his vision.

7 The next stop with the silent sergeant was the Navy Dispensary. Adam left all the gear in the back of the jeep, although the sergeant didn't think it was a good idea, and went into the dispensary ready, at last, to fight for his

rights and, at last, to put up some resistance to all this pushing around.

"I just had my annual physical," Adam told the young
doctor.

"Strip," the doctor said.

"There's nothing wrong with me," Adam argued. "I just
went through the whole physical two weeks ago."

"I know," the doctor said. "Strip."

"You medics think you know more about us than our
mothers," Adam said.

"We do. Strip."

There were two things, Adam remembered, that even the
Marines couldn't whip—the medical department and the pay
officer. He stripped down to his dog tags and the doctor
went to work on him. By the time Adam got through jumping up and down on one foot, saying "ah," giving with the
hollow cough, lying down, standing up, bending over, getting thumped, prodded and listened to, the doctor said,
"You're in pretty good shape—for an aviator. Okay, shots."

This was too much. "I just had all my shots, Doc. *All* of
'em."

"Shots," the doctor said, and began, first in one arm, then
the other. "All right," he said, at last, "put on your clothes
and come back here."

As Adam got dressed he had to admit now, to himself,
that when the C.O. ordered him confined to quarters it
shook him. Shook him bad. He couldn't remember doing anything particularly wrong; at least nothing wrong enough to
rate being confined, but he had heard stories of guys who
had talked a little too much or said something they weren't
supposed to say and *wham* they disappeared. There were
intelligence and security people all over the place. (He remembered the posters with the girl's face and the ships sink-

ing in the background and the line THIS MOUTH SANK THESE SHIPS.)

He'd been shook, but now, as this nonsense went on and on, he was sure that the whole thing was just a mistake. He wasn't in any real trouble. Somebody had just pulled the wrong name or the wrong serial number. Pretty soon they'd find out about it and, maybe, even apologize for ruining his day.

"Here's a first-aid kit for you," the doctor said.

"There's one in the plane," Adam said, thinking about the pile of gear he already had waiting for him in the back of the silent sergeant's jeep.

"You may not be in a plane," the doctor said. "And this one's a little different. Now, look, if you get shot don't fiddle around with the wound. If you think there's a bullet in you, leave it in there. Just sprinkle some of this powder around where it went in, and if it comes out, where it came out; don't wash it, no matter how dirty you think the place looks. Powder it, wrap it up and forget it. Now, this is for burns. Just smear it on, wrap it up and forget it. If you get around some spare water soak the bandages in that, too."

"I thought all this was what the medical department was for," Adam said.

"No," the doctor said, "we take care of bad colds, low back pains and athlete's foot. Now—how much pain can you stand? I mean by that, how much pain can you take and still function?"

"Doc, I don't know," Adam said helplessly. "I never had much pain, I guess."

"Well, let me put it this way: When the pain is so great that you don't think you can handle it, wait until it gets twice as great. If it does that, then use this. But, remember, this is morphine, a drug, and becoming a drug addict is a lot more painful than anything you'll get in combat. So don't use these things unless you think the pain is going to take you out. Now the rest of the kit is just common sense. A lot of people who get hit aren't killed by damage to something vital but by loss of blood. Try to stop that if you can. Or get your buddy to stop it for you." The doctor put the stuff carefully back into the canvas kit and handed it over to Adam.

"Don't I have to sign for it?" Adam asked.

"No, it's a gift from the grateful taxpayers. I hope you don't have to use it."

"Thanks. I'll take it along every time I go surfing in anything big."

"You do that," the doctor said, dismissing him.

Now, outside, it was dark—pitch-black dark, for every light in the Hawaiian Islands was blacked out except for dim, hooded lights on official vehicles. As Adam walked toward the dark waiting jeep he looked up toward Honolulu and could see nothing except black mountains with dark gray clouds gathered around their peaks. In the blackness you could not tell that a city crowded along the coast and spread up the sides of the mountains.

Adam was hungry now and remembered that all this foolishness had started before lunch—so he had missed that—and it was now well past dinner time. "Chow down, Sergeant, clear the mess decks. Let's go out to P. Y. Chong's and I'll buy you a steak dinner." Then he suddenly remembered that the Marine Corps had taken every dime he owned. "Belay that," he added, "the Marine Corps' got all my loot. So what are we going to do for chow, Sergeant?"

"Get in, Lieutenant," the sergeant said, starting the jeep.

Adam got in, tossing the first-aid kit into the back with the rest of the gear. "Home, James," he said.

8 The huge naval base at Pearl Harbor was weird in the wartime night. This night dark clouds were pouring down from the Pali. There were no moon, no stars, the sky and the earth were dark and there should have been silence in such darkness or, at most, only the small sounds of natural things in the night but, all around Adam as he sat in the slowly moving jeep, there were great sounds. Hammers were pounding on bent and twisted steel, the sound of their blows reverberating against the mountains. Riveting guns were slamming slugs of red-hot iron against the backup tools. Enormous saws, their blades running with oil, were cutting through armor plate and cranes were taking these slabs of steel and carrying them, whirling in the black sky, to some ship which needed them to patch a wound made by the enemy in some far off engagement.

Everything was dark and yet work was going on everywhere so that the night was filled with all manner of sound.

Other cars, moving as slowly and carefully as his, came out of the darkness, moved a moment, disappeared. Men on foot hurried from one dark place to another while above all this the planes of the air patrol could be heard high and hammering in the clouds.

Adam had long ago lost his bearings and now did not have any idea where he was except that it certainly wasn't the Marine Base at Ewa. He was still in Pearl Harbor because they had not been stopped at any gate, but none of the buildings were familiar to him now and, in the darkness, he could not even tell what types of ships were moored in the harbor.

Adam was beginning now to get a little worried. It was well known that the Marine Corps moved in mysterious ways its wonders to perform but it was not absolutely unheard of for the corps to make a mistake. And dressing him up like this and loading him down with useless junk and carting him around in the dark of night was about the biggest mistake the Marine Corps had made since it allowed the Navy to take it over.

"You sure you got the right party, Sergeant? I'm just a happy pilot."

"I got the right party, Lieutenant," the sergeant said in his talkative way.

"Then what's this all about?" Adam asked, hungry now and irritable. "What am I supposed to do with all this junk? Who am I supposed to shoot with that greasy gun back there? Or who am I supposed to stab with that greasy dagger?"

For the first time the sergeant explained things a little. "I imagine, Lieutenant, that your targets will be targets of opportunity, sir."

"Come on!" Adam said, "I got the dagger and you got the cloak so let's get together here."

The jeep stopped and the sergeant said, "End of the line, Lieutenant."

"Now wait a minute," Adam said firmly. "I'm a long way from home. It's after curfew so there're no taxis—and I couldn't pay one if there were. So what do you mean, end of the line? I've got to get back to my squadron. After all, Sergeant, I'm in the Armed Forces too and I have duties and things like that."

"You can say that again," the sergeant said. "So long, Lieutenant. Good luck."

Adam made no move to get out of the jeep. "I've got some pals out in the squadron with a real odd-ball sense of humor. If this is part of it let's don't let 'em get away with it."

"This is as far as I go," the sergeant said, turning off the ignition and taking the key out.

It made Adam mad. "All right. Now wait a minute. How do I get back to my squadron?"

"You don't, Lieutenant."

"I do, Sergeant. So far I've gone along with this gag but now I want to see something official. You come along and say 'Get in.' Then you say 'Get out.' 'Get in. Get out.' And I wind up with a bunch of toys and a union suit in the middle of Pearl Harbor in the middle of the night. So, now, who're you?"

The sergeant got out of the jeep without saying a word, walked around the back of it and came up on Adam's side where he stood in the darkness. He stood up straight, with his legs a little apart and the big gun hanging at his hip. "Personally," the sergeant said, "I'm nobody. But when I get orders from the Commander in Chief, Pacific Fleet, to bring Lieutenant Adam Land to Building Eight then I'm somebody. This is Building Eight, Lieutenant."

Adam had learned long ago how useless—and dangerous—it was to argue with a marine doing his duty. Especially when he was armed. "Okay," Adam said, getting out of the jeep, "I'll just have to take this to higher authority."

"Your gear, Lieutenant," the sergeant said, pointing toward the back of the jeep.

At least the sergeant was polite enough to help him gather up all the stuff and arrange it so that he could carry it and move at the same time. Then the sergeant pointed to a closed door in the side of the building and got back into the jeep.

Adam struggled over to the door and banged on it with his knee, his hands being full at the time. Nothing happened, so at last he put down enough of the stuff to turn the knob. Beyond the door was the blackest darkness he had ever seen. It made the dark night around him look like high noon.

Gathering up his stuff again, he went into the blackness and closed the door. For a moment he stood in total blackness and then brilliant light came on and he saw, just ahead of him, another door.

Adam opened this and entered a bleak, narrow corridor with, in front of him, another sergeant sitting at a little wooden desk with a gooseneck lamp on it. Adam went over to him and rested some of the gear on the desk. "I'm Lieutenant Land, attached to Bombing Six and I need transportation out there."

The sergeant checked a list on the desk in front of him and pointed down the corridor. "Third door on your left, Lieutenant."

"Transportation?" Adam asked.

For the first time the sergeant really raised his head and looked at him. "Transportation, Lieutenant," he said, and turned the list face down on the desk.

Adam went down the long hall, the boondockers pounding hollowly on the rough wood floor, the various items of his gear clinking and clanking together as he walked and the starched cloth creaking. The third door to his left was a plain, cheap door with no writing on it. It had never been painted either, so that the area around the knob had been stained by many hands. Adam opened it completely so that he could get in without his gear jamming and came into a long bleak room. The only lights were two hanging fixtures with white enameled shades, the enamel chipped with the metal rusting through it. The bulbs could not have been more than twenty-five watts apiece so that the long barren room was dimly lit.

It was a depressing place. The wooden walls had never been paneled so he could see the tar paper on the outside. The roof rafters were open and a good many spiders seemed to live up there. There were three little windows, closed tight and covered with black cloth.

A narrow, hard, wooden bench was nailed to three walls of the room and that was the only furniture in the place.

It didn't look much like a motor pool or transportation office and Adam stood in the doorway looking at the marines sitting on the benches. There were about twenty of them, all dressed as he was in the two-piece fatigues and, like him, without any sign of rank or rate. They might have all been generals.

Somebody said, "Shut the door."

"Transportation?" Adam asked.

"Shut the door."

Adam shut the door and said, "I need transportation back to base."

The men looked at each other, amused, and one of them said, "Ain't that the truth."

"Look," Adam said, "I'm in enough trouble with my C.O. already. I don't need another out-after-curfew."

"Relax," one of the men said. "You'll get your transportation. And if what I think is right you'll have transportation up to *here*."

"You guys waiting for transportation, too?" Adam asked.

"That's what we're waiting for."

Adam clinked and clanked his way over to a deserted stretch of the bench and sat down, leaning the rifle against the bench. It slid slowly down and then fell on the floor.

Every man in the place straightened up and looked at the carbine lying on the floor. They kept on looking at it until it made Adam uncomfortable. He picked it up and laid in on the bench. This disturbed his pile of gear. First a canteen rolled off the bench and hit with a hollow but dead noise, rolled a little way, then stopped. After that came the other canteen, the mess kit and, in the silent room, it made

an odd, long noise, the utensils inside the aluminum kit rattling around long after it hit the floor. Then the helmet
teetered on the edge of the bench for a while and at last
fell with a great clang and spun around.

Adam picked the stuff up piece by piece and got them
balanced on the bench.

Now he was not only hungry, he was frazzled and frus-
trated. He had had the dawn patrol, with a 4 A.M. takeoff,
then the long gunnery flight, then all this foolishness. But he
had been in the Navy long enough to know that when
they told you to wait there was absolutely nothing you could
do but wait. There was no way to shorten the time of waiting, no way to avoid it. Wait.

He wondered now if any marine had ever been told to
wait some place and then been forgotten by whoever told
him to wait. Maybe there were ancient marines scattered
all over the world still waiting. Their beards would be down
to their navels, their rifles (maybe old muzzle-loaders?) rusting away, grass growing up through their shoes—but still
waiting.

Adam leaned back against the bare studs of the wall and
looked, without any interest at all, around the room.

Now that he had gotten used to the two dim light bulbs
he could see the men on the benches more clearly and, as
he now looked at them, they began to impress him.

These were not ordinary men, and for a while Adam could
not make up his mind as to what made them different from
any other bunch of twenty men but, slowly, he began to find
things that distinguished these guys.

For one thing, they were the most honed-down bunch of
people he had ever seen. They were bone-thin (but not
skinny); so lean the bones of their faces were clear and their
hands seemed to grow out from leather-covered bones.
When they moved it was a smooth thing to watch for these

men were balanced in their movements and co-ordinated.

Their faces were different, one from another, and yet, in a way, all the same. Thin, with a certain tenseness around their mouths and, although they were all young (Adam guessed that the oldest man in the room wasn't over twenty-five), they seemed much older. Their eyes were old, Adam decided. There was something in the look of their eyes that made you feel that they were old; that they had seen things you would never see.

He wondered what made these people so different from, say, the pilots in his squadron. They were about the same age—late teens, early twenties—and came from the same places, Detroit, Ocala, New York, Little Rock. Of course these marines looked *harder* than the pilots and Adam thought that this look, perhaps, came from the better physical condition of the marines. The pilots weren't in bad shape, but they did not compare to the leaned-out, whit-leather look of these men.

And then it struck him that these marines had a thing the pilots did not have at all. And the only word he could find to describe it was "dangerous." These guys looked dangerous. Not mean, not menacing. Just dangerous.

Somehow, too, they were older. They seemed to know who they were and why and Adam knew very well that, at one time or another, every pilot (including him) had suddenly asked himself, "What am I doing *here?* What am I, Joe Doe, doing in this airplane getting ready to go to war. I don't know anything about war. I don't know anything about killing anybody. What am I *doing* here.

But these marines in this bleak room didn't ask themselves that. They, Adam knew, had been to war, and were now waiting to go again.

Then he noticed something that surprised him. Each man in the room had exactly the same assortment of junk he had. The gun, helmet, canteen, mess kit, ammo, first-aid, camouflage grease, pouches, dagger—all of it—and yet, when you looked at them you didn't see it. His gear was spread along the bench for a yard on each side of him; their gear was so co-ordinated with them you didn't notice it. They looked as though they had always gone around carrying all this junk, that it was part of them.

They began to interest him and he sat on the bench and watched them, noticing first this thing and then that. For one thing, he noticed that every one of them held on to his rifle *all* the time and held it not as you would a shovel but as something vital to you. The rifles were always moving as the men held them and worked the bolts or cleaned them or tinkered in one way or another with them.

Another thing Adam noticed was that the men seemed divided into pairs. They were more or less spaced along the bench in pairs. They talked together in pairs and, if something two of them were talking about interested some others they would talk about it, all together, but briefly, and then go back to the pair thing.

There was no loud talking; even the laughter was short and quiet. By focusing on one or two of them at a time Adam could pick out a single conversation from the low murmur of the total talk.

"Willie said to the mess cook, 'What you got in that pot?' and the mess cook said, 'Boiled bats,' and Willie said, 'Oh, I thought it was something I couldn't eat.'"

A man across the room asked, "Where'd Willie get it?"

"In the river. He managed to crawl up on a sand bar but we couldn't get out there to him. They had it *covered*."

The man across the room said, "Oh, was that Willie? I saw a guy out there but I didn't know who it was."

Adam focused on another pair. "What do you *know!*" one of them said, surprised. "This is my birthday."

"Yeah? How old are you?"

"Twenty-five."

"You *old!*"

"I don't *feel* so old."

"You gonna feel old."

Another was saying, "I didn't take off my shoes for eight days and when I took 'em off you know my socks had rotted clean away. Just rotted clean away."

"With these socks they give us it's a wonder your toes didn't rot off too. They're sure lousy socks."

Another man could hardly tell the story for laughing. "These snipers were all up in the palm trees and we were banging away, everybody. The Garands and BARs and the light MGs. Man, it sounded like Gene Krupa on a wild rip and we weren't hitting a thing and then sarge came along and said, 'Stop making so much fuss.' So we quit shooting and he slung that old ought-three around, fiddled with the windage a little and, then, right in the middle of this little path, he got down in the kneeling position like he was instructing raw recruits and started shooting that old iron . . . pow . . . pow . . . pow. And I tell you they were falling out of those trees like coconuts."

"The oh-three can shoot all right. I don't say you can't hit with it. But I want something that *pours* it out."

"I don't know," the other one said, dubiously. "I like the Garand all right. But look how many of the old timers still tote that oh-three."

"They're the sharpshooters. The five-hundred-yard boys," the first one argued. "But when they come at you the way they did on the Ridge that morning I want Garands and BARs. *Pouring* it out!"

Across the room a long, lean man with a nose like a beak had his back against the wall, his long legs stretched out into the room, his rifle lying across his lap. "That kid used to tickle me," he was saying. "Every time they sent him up to the line he'd steal a towel from somewhere and the lieutenant would say, 'Hey, you don't need a towel where you're going.' And the kid would say (you remember how mild a guy he was, real mild talking), 'Well, maybe I will, Lieutenant,' and he'd go on with the gun and as soon as he was out of sight of the lieutenant he'd throw the tripod away and the three of 'em, without that tripod catching in everything, could really *move*. And they could start shooting faster than any MG team in the business."

"Was he the one hand-held that gun?" the next man asked.

"That's the one. I forget his name, he was a Pfc. But he'd wrap that towel around the barrel of the gun and *hip*-fire it. It'd ride up on him, naturally, so he couldn't get off anything but short bursts but what difference did that make? When he could drive *nails* with that gun."

"Where'd he get it?"

"I don't think he did. I heard he got in a tight with the gun up on some ridge where there was no water to wet that towel with and the canteens were dry and he'd thrown away the tripod so he just stood there and hip-fired the gun until the barrel burned through the towel and like to burned his hand off. Maybe they sent him home."

"You see those marks?" another one asked, holding out his rifle to the man next to him. The man looked and said, "The sergeant's going to get on you about that."

"He already has," the first one said. "But those are teeth marks."

The second man laughed and said, "Boy, bring me my sea boots. It's rising from the ground."

"Those are teeth marks," the other insisted. "We were crossing one of those little rivers, I forget the name, and the captain said to hold fire until we got all the way across, no matter what happened, so I'm halfway across and going real good when I look up—the water is right up to my chin—and there's this crocodile going to bite my head off. If the captain hadn't said 'Hold your fire' I could've put the gun down his mouth and blown all his brains out.

"So there we were in the middle of the river, me and this crocodile. You know something funny? The inside of a crocodile's mouth is white as a sheet. Real clean-looking. And I was thinking well, anyway, my head won't get some sort of infection when it gets in there. And something else funny, there was a little bird sitting on that crocodile's head laughing up a storm at the whole situation. So when the crocodile chomped down I put the rifle butt in his mouth. That's where his teeth went in the wood. Imagine what would have happened if he'd got hold of my head."

"He'd have broken his teeth," the other man said.

Adam waited to find out what happened to the crocodile but found, instead, that these marines and airplane pilots had one thing in common, they never finished the story. "There I was at thirty thousand feet, over on my back, with no propeller and no parachute and both wings shot off. So what's new?"

Adam asked the room at large, "When did they say they'd get that transportation around here?"

"They didn't say," someone told him and another said, "'They also serve who only stand and wait.'"

Adam looked at the gear scattered around him on the bench and finally made up his mind. There'd been a mistake somewhere but he'd been in the Navy long enough to know that the Navy takes care of the guy who takes care of himself. He got up, leaving all the gear on the bench and walked across the room toward the door. Some of the marines looked up at him and Adam said, "I think I'm in the wrong group."

"Aren't we all?" one of the men said.

Adam opened the door and had taken one step out into the hall when, from nowhere, another of these leaned-out marines with a rifle appeared, standing directly in front of him with the muzzle of the rifle one inch from Adam's naval.

"Where do you think you're going?" the marine asked.

"Look, friend," Adam said, "this is a foul-up of some sort. I've got to get some transportation."

"You got some transportation," the marine said.

"That's what I mean," Adam told him. "I don't know where those guys are going, but I've got to see a man about a real *big* dog, and I got to do it *now!*"

"All I know is—you guys are all present and accounted for and I'm going to keep it that way. Back in your hole!" He pushed Adam with the rifle back toward the room.

"Then let me make a phone call."

"No phone calls."

"Look, buddy," Adam said, getting irritated, "I'm the wrong man in the wrong place at the wrong time. I've got to get word to my commanding officer where I am and what's going on or I'll be in *big* trouble."

"You tell *him*—or anybody else—where you are and you're going to be in *huge* trouble. Back in the hole!"

"I'm a lieutenant in the United States Navy," Adam said, at last angry, "and I want to make an official, government business, essential-to-the-war-effort telephone call to my commanding officer. You got any objections to that?"

"And I'm General MacArthur. So don't give me any more trouble, buster. My orders are for you guys to stay in that room. So that's where you're going to stay." He patted the rifle menacingly.

Adam, defeated again, went back into the bleak room, made a space in his junk and sat down. As far as he could tell, the other men didn't even know he was there.

Adam tried now to put his problem into some sort of form

so he could solve it. That a mistake had been made some-where was evident and it was the sort of mistake that just kept getting worse and worse until, if you didn't straighten it out, you wound up in a naval prison, or the hospital, or even dead.

To appeal for help to the lean men around him was, he decided, useless. They were some sort of club, or secret society, or something and he wasn't a member and they weren't beginning to ask him to join up.

To try to get past the marine with the rifle at the door would solve his problem in one of two ways—he'd wind up in the hospital with a bullet in him, or he would wind up lying on the floor of this place dead.

He was still struggling with the thing when one of the marines got up off the bench and started walking across the room toward him. Adam had noticed this one before mainly because, unlike the others, he had been sitting by himself, apart from all the others, and hadn't said a word. Now he was walking toward Adam carrying his rifle at the trail, his helmet on but the chin strap dangling, all his gear hanging from the metal loops on the belt and the belt looking as though it were going to slide right down his almost hip-less body. None of the stuff clinked or clanked and, on the man, it seemed weightless. It also looked as though it belonged there.

The man was dangerous. Right here in some building in Pearl Harbor, Hawaii, in a quiet, depressing room, the man was dangerous. Not, Adam decided, to you, personally. Not the way a bully is dangerous. Nor a mad dog. He was just a man who, when a situation called for violence, knew how to use violence with great and controlled efficiency. He was dangerous.

He stopped in front of Adam, the helmet throwing a deep shadow on his face so Adam could hardly see it, and stood a moment looking down at Adam, his rifle at a sort of parade rest angle.

Maybe, Adam suddenly hoped, this was the officer in charge, or something. The boss. Now he could explain the mistake and get out of here. That's all—get out of *here*. Then he could get this mess straightened out.

"My name's Jason," the man said.

The voice startled Adam. From the menace of the tall man with his face in shadow Adam had expected a deep, rough voice, full of authority. This voice was timid and so young that it was not yet under full control.

"I'm Adam Land," Adam said.

The man shifted his rifle over to his left hand and held out his right hand. As they shook hands Adam noticed that the palm and fingers of Jason's hand felt like rough, dry wood. "You a marine?" Jason asked.

"What's a marine? Listen, are you in charge of this bunch?"

"Me? In charge? I'm only a corporal."

There went that hope, shot down. "Who *is* in charge?"

"I don't know. Nobody yet, I guess." He moved toward the bench and then hesitated and asked, his voice breaking a little. "Mind if I sit down?"

"Help yourself," Adam said, surprised.

Jason sat down, none of his gear banging against anything, and then started talking. It sounded to Adam as though he were talking mostly to himself. "My buddy got it," Jason said. "It surprised me."

He turned to look at Adam, the helmet still shading his face so that Adam could see only the vague shape of it. "I mean, I'd seen a lot of guys get it. There was nothing new about that. But they were . . . well, they were *other* guys. Brooks was my buddy. We went through boot camp together and tank school and everywhere. Me and Brooks, you see. We hit the beach in the same boat and everything. So I guess what surprised me was that it was closer than some other guy getting it." He turned to look at Adam again. "You know, I couldn't believe it. For a long time I just sat there in the foxhole and didn't believe it. Brooks was always clowning around. Don't get me wrong, he was the *best* in a fire fight, but he would clown around. So, I thought, maybe he's got tomato catsup spread all over and is clowning around." Jason raised his head and looked up at the light bulb. "He wasn't," he said.

Adam could now see his face clearly. Jason was only a kid. A kid right now on the verge of crying, with his lips tight together to keep from it and his eyes blinking it away.

Then he lowered his head again and fiddled with the rifle. Suddenly he laughed. Not loud, just a low, short laugh. "They think I'm a kook or something," Jason said, looking out from under the helmet at the other men in the room. "In boot camp I thought I'd get a medal right away. I've been shooting guns since I was knee-high to a grasshopper and I thought, 'Put me out on that range with a gun and I'll get a medal right now.' Well, I went out there and they gave me an M-1 and showed me all about it and I shot it." He looked at Adam and said seriously, "You know, I couldn't hit the broad side of a barn with the doors shut with that gun. I just couldn't. I didn't even *qualify*. It was pretty bad," he said. "What made it worse was that I'd told all these guys, Brooks and all of them, what a hot-shot rifle shot I was and how I'd show 'em how it ought to be done. Well. . . ."

Adam wondered if this was going to be another no-end marine story, but then Jason went on. "So this old gunnery sergeant came up to me and said, 'Marine, you're going to learn how to handle that rifle if I have to weld it on to you.' You know how they go on, eating you out right up to the ears, but while he was eating me out I was looking at the rifle he had and I said, 'Sergeant, what kind of gun is that?' and he blew his stack, naturally, because I opened my mouth when he was talking and said, 'That's a gun for men, not boys.' But it was a gun like I'd been shooting all my life so I said, 'Let me fire a couple of rounds with your gun, Sarge.'"

Jason laughed the short, low laugh again. "Maybe you've seen a mad sergeant but this one was the maddest in the Marine Corps. He got about nine feet tall and red all over. Smoke shot out of his ears and flames out of his nose and his voice sounded like it was coming through some gravel. Brooks, who was standing there beside me, said he thought I was going to be burned down to a little crisp. The sergeant went on like that for about ten minutes saying, mainly, that no wet-behind-the-ears useless raw punk recruit was going to lay so much as a finger on his rifle and for me to have a thought like that should get me ten days on bread and water. So when he got through and calmed down a little, I said, 'Just a couple rounds, Sarge.' Then he blew again and explained that if I didn't shoot a toy gun like the Garand how did I expect to shoot a real gun like the 1903 Springfield rifle. 'Just a couple rounds, Sarge,' I said."

Jason held up his rifle. "I've been shooting that old ought-three ever since. The guys think I'm a kook. Brooks even thought I was a kook. But I can shoot this gun and with the Garand I couldn't blow the bottom out of a beer can with the muzzle stuck in the top."

"Any teeth marks on it?" Adam asked.

Jason looked at him with startled surprise. "How'd you know that?" he asked.

"Crocodiles," Adam said.

"Oh, no, that was Smitty with that crocodile. No, Brooks and I were in a hole one night and these crazy guys rushed us. You know the way they do, come jumping and yelling. I guess they think all that noise is going to scare you. Anyway, I was changing clips and one of them came for Brooks and all I could do was swing the oh-three like a baseball bat. Those are his teeth marks."

Adam looked at him again. He had a clean, lean, innocent face with dark blue eyes which still had the surprised look of youth in them. Adam wondered about him.

Jason laughed again. "They're nuts," he declared. "One night on Bloody Ridge they started yelling 'We hate Babe Ruth.' In English, they were yelling it. Like a chorus. 'We hate Babe Ruth.' I asked the sarge what that was all about and he said they were doing it to infuriate us. To make us so mad we'd start shooting or attacking them or something. So I asked the sarge, 'Who's this Babe Ruth?' and I really thought he was going to break down and cry. He said, 'How can the Marines win a war with kids that don't even know who Babe Ruth is! There ought to be a *law!*' Sergeants!" Jason said. "I'm dying for a little sleep, me and Brooks (he didn't know who Babe Ruth was either) but the sergeant wouldn't let us. He kept us awake all night telling us who Babe Ruth was—how many times he went to bat, how many home runs he hit, what his batting average was for every year he played ball. I tell you, before he got through I was ready to go over on their side and join in singing 'We hate Babe Ruth.' What outfit you in, Land?"

"Bombing Six."

"Bombing Six? What's that?"

"Dive-bomber squadron."

Jason looked at him a little skeptically. "You an airedale?"

"I've been accused of it."

"Is that a combat squadron?"

"Not yet. But we have hopes."

"Oh," Jason said. Adam could feel any respect Jason may

have had for him falling away like autumn leaves. Although Jason didn't physically move it was as though he had moved about ten feet down the bench and into another world.

Now Jason slowly turned his head, the helmet shadowing his eyes, and looked for a long time at Adam before he asked, "Are you an officer?"

Adam nodded.

"Oh," Jason said. Then he got up without looking at Adam again and walked across the room and sat down all by himself on the bench. He put the rifle across his lap, pushed his feet out along the floor, let his head, still in the helmet, drop.

He looked so lonely.

9 It was one o'clock in the morning when another of the lean marines came into the room. He had on the same outfit as the rest of them but Adam was sure that he was an officer. "All right, gentlemen," the man said, "and away we go."

Adam went over to him, his helmet rolling off the bench again, and said, "Sir, there's been a mistake. I'm a naval aviator attached to VB-6. I'm a lieutenant but somehow I've gotten lashed up in this deal and I can't get out. Nobody knows where I am and they won't let me even call my C.O. Maybe you can get me straightened out."

"Oh yes," the officer said, looking at a list of names on a piece of paper. "You must be Lieutenant Land."

Oh, boy! Oh, joy! Adam thought, at last somebody is making some sense around here. "There must be another Adam Land—in the Marine Corps."

"Perhaps," the officer said.

"Is it okay to leave all this junk here? And could I get

some sort of official note so I won't get in trouble for being out after curfew?"

"Here's an official note," the officer said, handing Adam some papers.

"Thanks," Adam said, glancing at the typewritten paragraphs. Then he looked at them again, staring, not believing what he read. It was all there in the first short paragraph:

"1. Lieutenant Adam Land is hereby detached from VB-6 and will proceed immediately and report to Commander Operation Moondance in whatever port he may be for duty on his Staff."

"They've got the wrong man!" Adam said.

"Okay, gentlemen, fall in," the officer said.

The marines silently got up from the bench and formed into two ranks. The man with the birthday was at the head of them and now asked, "Is this going to be another dirty one, Major?"

"Could be," the major said. "Let's go."

As Adam stood there, not believing the words he was reading, the marines walked out of the room.

Adam was still standing there as the last one came by. "Here's your gear, sir," the kid, Jason, said, his arms full of Adam's paraphernalia.

"What's this all about?" Adam asked. "Where're we going? Come *on*, what's it all about?"

"They don't ever tell you, sir. Not even after you hit the beach. I didn't know I was on Guadalcanal until after I left the place. They called that Operation Watchtower."

"Are we going to some *island?*" Adam asked, really alarmed now. "Look, I can't go. I'm not supposed to."

"Come on, you guys," the major said. "March!"

As the marines went silently down the hall toward the door, Adam hurried until he caught up with the major. "Sir, something is all fouled up! I'm a pilot. An aviator. They've got the wrong name, or something."

"Did you read your orders?"

"Yeah, but somebody must've made a mistake!"

"There's no mistake, Lieutenant, so let's go. Shall we?"

Here it is again, Adam thought. Some general makes a mistake in a name or a serial number and then the giant machine takes over and you're caught in The System. His only hope, he knew now, was to go along with this thing until he could get to somebody with real authority—a colonel or, maybe, even a general, and get this mess straightened out.

Adam fell in at the end of the column where Jason was walking, still carrying Adam's gear. Adam slipped his arm through the helmet chin strap, then relieved Jason of the rifle and as much of the other stuff as he could carry.

Outside, the clouds from the Pali had swept down low over Pearl Harbor. It was so dark and so close to raining that it was hard even to make out the road they were walking along and the buildings on each side were just blacker parts of the cloud.

There was no talking. You could hear the boondockers on the asphalt and, occasionally, the clink of a canteen or something, but the column, to Adam, seemed dark and silent. "I wonder where we're going?" Adam whispered to Jason.

"Ssh!" Jason said and then added a whispered, "sir."

They walked for a long way and at last Adam knew that they had reached a dock or a wharf because, beyond it, he could hear water lapping against something.

"Detail," the major called quietly, "halt."

The men ahead of Adam stopped in the dark and he heard the rifle butts being lowered gently to the ground.

"At ease," the major said, "but no talking. The smoking lamp is out."

Ahead of him Adam could see the outlines of the men, still in ranks, but now relaxed and moving a little. There was no sound here except the lap of water against something and the far away sounds of riveting.

He was standing there thinking that this was like those nightmares in which something was forcing you to move when to move meant falling over a cliff. In the dream you knew that all you had to do was find out what the force was and fight it but you couldn't find out. This was the same, he decided. But there *must* be a force; there must be an officer somewhere to whom he could appeal; the Secretary of the Navy; the President. Or he would go over the cliff.

Then, as he stood there in the darkness in his own nightmare, something grabbed him.

Adam was so startled he dropped the two canteens which, fortunately, were in the canvas covers, so only made thudding sounds when they hit.

Jason had him by the arm, his fingers digging into Adam's muscles. "Oh no!" Jason was saying in a terrified whisper. "Oh no! Oh no!"

"Turn loose," Adam whispered. "What's the trouble?"

"It's a submarine!" Jason said. Adam couldn't see his face in the darkness but in the tone of his voice and by his movements Adam knew that this kid in his combat outfit was terrified.

"They can't put me on a submarine," Jason wailed. "I can't go down in any submarine. I just can't do it!"

"I can't either," Adam said, "but it sure looks like we're going to."

"You're an officer," Jason said, pleading. "You can do something. Tell them I can't go in a submarine. Tell them if I have to go in a submarine I won't be able to fight." Then he said, in a small voice, "I'm sick, Lieutenant."

"Then get well, buddy," Adam told him.

"But you're an *officer!*"

"I'm nobody at all," Adam said, and, suddenly, he realized that this was true. Adam Land, lieutenant, navy pilot, ace surfboard rider, the man voted by his high school class as Most Likely to Become a Playboy, didn't seem to exist any more. In his place was a nameless person of no character or distinctness—a person in a dream—standing in the dark with his arms full of things he did not know how to use. Standing there waiting his turn to get down into this submarine and go to some unknown place where he had no business to be.

"I just can't go in a submarine," Jason cried.

"Pipe down!" the major said and added, "All right, gentlemen, one at a time."

Ahead of Adam a marine with the deepest southern drawl Adam had ever heard whispered. "This heah's a plot bah the Navy. They gonna revenge theyselfs."

"I'm afraid," Jason whispered. "Just the idea of going under water in that thing makes me sick at my stomach."

"Stay loose," Adam told him. "If the Navy can do it, we can."

"But it might not come up!"

"They know how to get it up again," Adam told him, and hoped they did.

The line of men was moving steadily forward and now Adam and Jason had reached the gangplank leading down to the deck of the submarine. In the dark the ship looked black and menacing, a long, flat-topped, low ship. The conning tower, black and streamlined, rose above him and he could see the outlines of men up there leaning over the high shield looking down at them as the marines moved steadily forward and disappeared, one by one, down the forward hatch.

As Adam and Jason passed the shrouded deck gun a

truck on the dock started its motor and began to move off. On its flatbed Adam could make out the shapes of torpedoes lying in wooden cradles. The truck, with no lights, drove on away into the darkness.

"I don't want to go," Jason said, his voice childish and frightened.

"It won't be so bad," Adam told him, feeling a little ashamed of himself because he knew that *he* wasn't going anywhere in this terrifying boat. "At least the enemy can't see you in a submarine."

"But it's *under* the water!" Jason cried.

"All right, gentlemen, down you go," the major said.

Ahead of him, just around a blacker place in the deck Adam could see the head and shoulders of a man disappearing downward and when he was gone he waited, touching Jason on the arm. "Go ahead," he said.

Jason walked toward the hatch like a man walking to be hanged. He turned his face back to Adam and asked, plaintively, "Are you coming, too . . . sir?"

"Right behind you," Adam said.

He waited until Jason disappeared into the black hole and then, awkward with all the gear, moved forward and searched for the rungs of the ladder he could not see.

There was one good thing about all this, Adam thought, as he climbed down, his gear clanging and banging against things as he moved. Whoever was really in charge of this outfit would be aboard the submarine. Once in the thing he was going straight to the boss and explain that his being here was a mistake. He wasn't going to be pushed around in this thing any more. Not by sergeants or majors or colonels or even generals. Somebody had made a mistake and since nobody else seemed ready to straighten it out he'd do it himself.

"You're standing on my head," a voice said from the dark

below him and Adam lifted his foot and then felt around with it until he could touch the deck.

"Okay," somebody said, "all our little heroes are aboard, so close the hatch."

Somebody crowding against Adam in the dark moved and Adam could see him going up the ladder he had just come down. In a moment the black circle of the hatch cover swung down and then it was absolutely pitch-dark.

"Just what I thought," a voice said, "the Navy hires moles to run these things."

"Hit the lights," a voice ordered and brilliant lights came on.

Adam had never seen so many people in such a small place. With the lights on he found that he was being pressed back against what he guessed was the inner end of a torpedo tube. A big brass handle of some sort was up against his backbone but when he tried to move there was nowhere to go—the room was completely filled with marines, wall to wall.

"Whoever's standing on mah foots, get off," the southerner said, "so's ah can get off the foots ah'm standin' on."

"When are you going to learn to speak English, Rebel?" a voice asked. "You're not standing on my *foots*, you're standing on my *feets*."

"You ol' Yankee professor, *you*," the southerner said.

Adam squirmed around, trying to get the handle out of his backbone, and pushed up against the major who, in turn was trying to find a little room to breathe. "I've got to see the officer in charge, Major," Adam said. "Right away." He said it firmly and in a tone that would not allow refusal.

"Be my guest," the major said. "He's in this boat somewhere."

"What's his name?"

"Colonel Marcus."

Adam turned to Jason, who was standing perfectly still in front of him. In the bright light Jason looked gray and sick with his lips pressed together and his eyes closed. "Hold this stuff for me, will you, Jason?" Adam asked, pushing his rifle toward him.

Jason's eyes snapped open and he said, "Where're you going? You going to get off? Get me off too."

"I'll be right back," Adam said, ashamed again for telling such a lie. But what could he do for Jason? It was going to be hard enough getting out of his own troubles and there wasn't a chance of getting Jason out of his. After all, Adam argued, Jason was a combat marine and had orders to be where he was. No aviation lieutenant was going to change that.

"Gangway," Adam said. "Excuse me. Gangway." Marines shoved and jostled and griped as he made his way through the pack of them. "Gangway. Gangway," he kept saying.

"What do you want me to do," the tall beak-nosed one asked, "vanish?" But he moved somehow enough for Adam to pass him and go on toward the closed door at the far end of the room.

At last he reached the door—if that's what it was called. It was a low, oval-shaped hole in the steel wall and he had to step up and over to get out of the crowded room.

The corridor he stepped into seemed just as crowded. It was a very narrow, low-ceilinged corridor jammed with people but here everyone was moving either one way or the other.

The people here were all Navy and Adam stopped the first one with a chief petty officer's cap and asked, "Where can I find Colonel Marcus?"

"In the skipper's stateroom," the chief said, making way for Adam to pass.

"Where's that?"

"Third door on your left."

"Thanks," Adam said.

"For nothing, hero," the chief said and went away.

As Adam struggled on down the narrow corridor he heard diesel engines start and felt the ship begin to quiver. He had better hurry, he thought, pushing past a sailor with a foot-long beard.

He heard a faint voice from the outer world say, "Take in four." And now, with the diesels idling, the ship was full of their sound—a low, panting hum.

"Take in one," the voice from outside ordered. "All back full."

Adam was feeling panicky now as the sound of the diesels grew stronger and he thought he felt a movement through the boat.

Hurry! Hurry! Adam thought, reaching the door at last and knocking hard on it.

"Come in," a voice told him.

As Adam stepped inside the room he was amazed. This was the stateroom of the submarine's commanding officer— no doubt a commander in the Navy—and the place wasn't as big as the closet in his room in bachelor officer's quarters. It was a tiny room with a thin, narrow bunk suspended by chains from the wall, a little toy desk, a little washbasin that was now folded up into the wall. And that was about all.

A thin man, very small and wiry-looking, was studying some charts spread out on the narrow bunk. He turned as Adam came in and stood so that the charts could not be seen.

From a loudspeaker in the ceiling Adam heard a voice order, "Ahead one third, left full rudder."

"Yes?" the thin man asked.

"Colonel Marcus? I'm Lieutenant Adam Land, attached

to VB-6. There's been a mistake, sir. Please ask them to stop this boat right away so I can get off."

"Mistake?" the colonel snapped. "What sort of mistake?"

"My being here, sir. I'm a navy pilot and this is an infantry outfit. We haven't got much time, sir. The boat's underway now."

"I know that," the colonel said, his voice testy. "Now—you are Adam Land, aren't you?"

"Yes, sir . . ."

The voice from the loudspeaker interrupted Adam then. "Ahead standard, rudder amidships." Now Adam could hear the water slapping hard against the boat.

"You got your orders?"

"Yes, sir. Please, Colonel, ask them to stop."

Adam was dying. The boat was moving fast now, the waves slapping with an almost metallic noise against the bows.

The colonel went on. "Then there's no mistake, Lieutenant. You are attached to my command for temporary duty. Glad to have you with us."

Adam stared at him. He couldn't believe that this long nightmare was still going on and, now, didn't look as though it would ever stop. "I've got to stay?" Adam asked helplessly.

"Yes."

The colonel turned back to the charts on the bunk but Adam did not take the hint and go. He stood for a long moment and then asked, "Am I going into combat, sir?"

The colonel didn't even bother to turn around. "Probably," he said.

"Colonel," Adam said, "I don't know anything about combat. I've never been in combat. I don't even know how to shoot a rifle!"

The colonel turned around then and looked at him. "You'd better learn," he said.

BOOK TWO
The Deep, Dark Sea

1 The beak-nosed gunnery sergeant was singing, "Gloom and misery everywhere," he sang.

"You're no Caruso," a marine told him.

The beak-nosed marine stopped singing and looked at the other one. "Caruso's dead."

"So you be careful."

"Gloom and misery everywhere," Beak-nose sang.

And he was right, Adam decided. The misery anyway. This submarine had been designed to carry *exactly* seventy men in the crew and there were now seventy of the crew aboard, plus the twenty combat marines and two officers, plus, unfortunately, Adam Land.

During the first day at sea there had been a little awkwardness. Although he suspected that the colonel and the major (and the ship's officers) considered him a sort of inferior object, Adam was, by Act of Congress, an *officer* and was thus supposed to rate officer treatment. He was supposed to have "accommodations" according to his rank, to eat in the officer's wardroom and to live in "officer's country." However, when Adam told them that he would rather stay with the enlisted men Adam suspected that the other officers had been rather relieved. There was no room for him in officer's country; no bunk in any of the officer's state-rooms, no extra seat at the table which almost completely filled the tiny wardroom.

There was hardly any more room for him forward in the torpedo compartment with the marines. The steel room was designed to be the business end of this boat, not a hotel. At the forward end were the six torpedo tubes—three on each side, one above the other. The heavy round doors of the tubes with their levers and dials dominated the whole place and, just being there, closed, shining with oil, they carried menace. Because of the marines, the submarine was not carrying torpedoes on this mission, so the empty torpedo racks along the walls could now be used for a place for a man to sleep if he didn't mind the sharp steel of the racks cutting through the thin pads they called mattresses.

In addition to the torpedo racks there were some fold-down pipe bunks and there was, of course, the steel deck. Altogether there was room enough for about half of the ma-rines and half of the ship's company who usually lived there to lie down at one time. The rest had to stand up or, if they could manage it without stepping on anybody, get to the wall and lean against that.

At first the marines had been a little leery of Adam. In the first place, he wasn't a marine and if you weren't a ma-rine you were, with these people, nothing. In the second, he was an officer and so, according to the book, he had to be treated as an officer—yes, sir, no, sir, make room for the lieu-tenant. Adam didn't have to say much to put an end to all that. He just said, "My name's Adam Land and I'm going to live in here with you guys so let's make it easy on all hands."

Added to the discomfort, the crowding, the heat, the bad air and all the rest there was, in all the marines, a fear of the submarine itself. None of them had ever been in one before and the idea of being under the sea was repellent to them. This fear was not helped at all by the place they were in. Walled in all around by steel there was no escape from this place, no way for a man to go. If the sea came in here. . . .

For a long time after leaving Pearl Harbor the sub stayed on the surface, protected by the patrol planes flying out of the Islands. On the surface the boat was affected by the wave motion of the upper surface and rolled and pitched as other boats do in a heavy sea. This violent movement, added to the fear each man had of the moment when the boat would submerge, really got to the marines. One by one they got seasick and there was no place to get sick in except your helmet. Within an hour the torpedo room was a mess with dying marines lying all over the place (and each other), helmets rolling around and the few who were not sick being driven to it by the general foul-up.

Adam was surprised that Jason, who had seemed to be truly *afraid* of going under the water, was one of the few who didn't get sick and stayed on his feet, doing what he could to help his buddies.

By the time the sub passed beyond the protection of the patrol planes, only four marines were still on their feet and the rest of them were now absolutely sure that they were going to die. They looked forward to it because nothing could be worse than the condition they were then in.

There were sounds in the boat—the sound of the waves beating against the outside of it, sounds of voices over the loudspeaker in the torpedo room, sounds of the big diesels panting back aft somewhere and the smaller sounds of other motors and generators. Adam had grown used to them by now and so the sounds had passed out of his consciousness.

Then, suddenly, there was a brand-new sound so different from all the rest that it had no place among them. It came barking over the loudspeaker, loud and raucous, and was the sound of an old-fashioned automobile horn. "Ah-oo-gah. Ah-oo-gah."

"What is this, the freeway?" Adam asked. "Maybe we're going slow in the fast lane or something."

And then, from the loudspeaker, a voice said, quite calmly, "Rig out bow and stern planes."

"What's going on?" Jason asked and Adam could tell from his face that he suspected.

Then the voice said, "Clear the bridge."

Jason looked at Adam, his young eyes asking the question, and Adam said, "I guess so."

"Bridge clear?" the voice asked over the loudspeaker. "Everybody down?"

"Bridge clear," another voice answered.

"Secure the hatch," the first voice ordered.

"Hatch secured, sir."

"All right," the calm voice said, "let's take her down."

Voices began to pour through the speaker as Jason stood, staring at the speaker's metal grill as though it were human. Adam saw the muscles in Jason's jaw beginning to jump a little and his lips fell open as though he were awaiting the clap of doom.

"Flood negative. Flood safety."

"Close induction."

"Green board, sir. Green board!"

"Bleed air."

"Air in the boat, sir."

"Eight degrees down bubble."

"Easy on those bow planes. *Easy*, this is a deep ocean."

"Blow negative."

"Well done. All ahead one third."

Jason turned to Adam. "When are we going under the water?"

"I think we are already. It's riding smoother."

There was now no sense of motion at all. The boat seemed to be standing still, neither rolling nor pitching, nor anything else. Adam noticed now that the diesels had stopped and their sound had been replaced by the low, powerful humming of the electric motors. Everything seemed quieter, more peaceful.

"Is this all there is to it?" Jason asked, looking around as though expecting the dark sea to come rushing at him from everywhere.

"That's all there is," Adam said, "there ain't no more."

The southerner rose slowly from the tangled heap of seasick bodies and said, "Suh, it ain't no '*more*,' it's it ain't no '*mo*.'"

Now, as there was no more motion to disturb them the lean, sick marines began to recover.

The beak-nosed one sat up and looked around at the mess. "Gloom and misery everywhere," he began to sing.

As the long voyage dragged on the marines began to become people to Adam. They didn't stop being marines, but they began to have names and individual faces, tones of voice he could recognize, character.

Apparently the beak-nosed one was not only the highest in rank and so their leader; he was, as a man, their leader. Although he was congenial enough, even funny at times, he seemed to Adam to be a lonely man and spent most of his time by himself, his long frame stretched out somewhere, his eyes open but not apparently looking at you. His name was Gibbs but no one ever called him that. He was "Guns"

or "Gunny" to the Pfc's and corporals, the sergeants sometimes called him "Nose," but not often and always in a
friendly way. Like the rest of him, which was just long bone
and muscle, Guns had a long and muscular nose which ran
on a slight angle down his face, giving him a quizzical look
as though his head was always cocked to one side.

Guns was the only one of them all who *never* forgot that
Adam was an officer, the others would remember it occasionally or not at all, but Guns never forgot it. There was no
friction between Adam and Guns as there was between him
and a tech sergeant who seemed, from the first, to resent
Adam's being there. Guns even called him Adam and didn't
say "sir" or "the lieutenant," but Adam knew that he remembered.

The tech sergeant Adam did not like was a communicator,
a radio and field-phone expert who let you know it. His favorite story was how, in boot camp, the personnel man had
tried his best to get him to take flight training and become
a pilot and an officer but the tech had turned it down. His
favorite line was that he'd told the personnel people that he
wanted to shoot some bullets, not shoot the breeze in BOQ.
He wasn't openly hostile to Adam but he was the only one of
the twenty who needled Adam in a subtle way, using his
status as an enlisted man to protect himself from the officer.
His name was Wirtz but they called him "Strings."

And then there was the Rebel. Adam had known a surfer
who reminded him of the Rebel. A clown. A real clown,
but he was so good on a surfboard that he could be ridiculous on it and still ride it. He was so good that he made
surfing look simple and easy and some of the kelp-kickers
hanging around the beach declared that, by making it look
so simple (riding in backwards while he read a comic book
and stuff like that) other people tried to do it that way too
and broke their necks.

There was something unreal about the Rebel; in fact, Adam had about decided, everything was unreal. Even his name. For a deep-dyed southerner, Ezra Stiles was a funny name. And that southern drawl. Adam had heard a lot of southerners talk and he'd never heard one of them talk the way the Rebel did. Amos and Andy sounded like college profs compared to the Rebel. It was unreal.

The Rebel even looked unreal and even the Marine Corps hadn't been able to change that. He was handsome enough to be in the movies, with good features and cool, gray eyes with straight black eyebrows and lashes long enough for a girl. He was the only marine aboard who didn't look physically dangerous and yet Jason had told him one night on the cigaret deck that the Rebel was a holy terror in any sort of fight from an alley brawl to a fire fight in the lines. "Maybe it's because he doesn't lose his head," Jason decided. "Some guys fight as wild as the Rebel but his is sort of controlled. He just doesn't go spraying the landscape with ammo. Don't ever tangle with him," Jason advised.

"I'm strictly a no-loud-noise type," Adam had said.

"I've been wondering," Jason said. "How are you in a fight?"

"Terrific," Adam said.

Jason sounded skeptical. "Yeah?"

"Terrific. I've never been in a fight."

"*No* kind of fight?" Jason asked, surprised.

"No kind of fight." He could feel Jason looking at him in the dark.

"You didn't even fight kids when you were a kid?" Jason asked.

"There weren't any available," Adam said, thinking about when he was a kid.

"And you're running around dressed like a marine," Jason said, amazed. "Why?"

Adam laughed. "I've been trying to find that out myself."

"Especially in a deal like this," Jason said. "Because I think this is going to turn out to be real hairy."

"Then stop the boat and I'll get off," Adam said.

Jason was the easiest of them all to understand, and yet Adam wondered sometimes if he really understood even Jason. If Adam had had a younger brother, it would have been, he decided, a kid like Jason. A good clean-cut kid trying too hard to be a man.

Jason wanted to be an inventor. "I invented a rocket one time," he told Adam. "I wasn't but about four or five years old, I guess, and I stole some of my father's shotgun shells and took out the powder and put it in this rocket I'd invented. It almost blew the back of our house off but that rocket flew. It really did. It went way up."

Jason was a tinkerer, a mechanic. "You should have seen me driving around in a car when I was only twelve years old," he bragged to Adam one night. "I got this old jalopy out of a junk heap and got it to run but, of course, they wouldn't let me drive it. But I knew this guy who had a license so I put two steering wheels in the car and two sets of pedals and an extra accelerator. Then he could sit over in the driver's seat acting like he was driving and all the time *I* was driving. I think it bugged the cops."

Jason was a tank man. "I love tanks," he told Adam. "You get inside that tin can on wheels and it makes you feel pretty good. I wish we'd gotten tanks sooner at Guadalcanal. I don't like it in the lines, down on your belly in the mud with nothing to stop all those bullets. In the line the bullets go over you whining and whistling and grunting, but in a tank they just go *ping, ping, ping* and there's so much noise in there anyway you hardly hear them."

Jason, Guns, the tech sergeant from the Com Section, the Rebel, the corporal who, when he got out of the Marine

Corps, was planning to be an undertaker ("I won't have any problem with supply and demand," he explained) and was an expert on fortifications, the Pfc who wanted to be a forester, the Pfc who wrote a letter to his girl every night, knowing it wouldn't get mailed.

Marines. But, slowly, as the voyage went on, people.

"This place is not fit for man nor beast," a marine declared, wiping the sweat off his bare chest with his hands and flicking it down on the already soaking wet deck.

"That's the stomp-down truth!" the southerner said. "Ah'm gonna write a letter to mah congressman."

"You got a congressman?"

"Sho' Ah got a congressman."

"It's a pity you can't write."

"Ah can make a X," the southerner said.

Two of the days had passed and Adam wondered how many more there were going to be. He didn't think he could endure many more.

"You're not paying attention," Jason told him. "You've still got the attitude that this rifle is just a toy, Lieutenant. But one of these days you're going to be looking down the barrel and you're going to see one of 'em and then it's going to be you—or him. And this"—he patted the rifle—"is what decides who it's going to be. So, pay attention."

"Yassuh," Adam said, mocking the southerner. "Ah'm givin' you mah en-ti-ah attention."

"Lieutenant," the southerner said, "you talk like that in Dixie and they take you and dip you in a barrel of hot tar and then in a barrel of duck feathers and then set you on a pole and ride you back across the Mason-Dixon line."

"Yassuh, boss," Adam said. "Ah'm goin' straighten up and flah raght."

"No use tryin' to teach him nothing about no rifle, Jason," the southerner decided. "He got a meagah brain."

"Pay attention," Jason said, taking the rifle away from Adam and putting it to his shoulder. "Now whoever called it 'pull the trigger' didn't know any more about it than you do. You 'pull' it and you don't hit anything. You *squeeze* it. Not with just your finger. You squeeze it with all your fingers, with your whole hand, with your arm. Everything you are squeezes that trigger because that's when it counts."

"I know something better to squeeze than a trigger."

"But theah ain't none of 'em heah," the southerner said. "So you pay attention to Jason because it ain't just you shooting to save yo' life. It may be you shootin' to save *mah* life. That's what makes it so important."

"Now the next thing, Lieutenant," Jason said, "is remember you're shooting the *rifle,* not the *target.* These sights are little, just a little V here and a stick there, and they're close together. But the target's way out *there.* You just can't see all three things clearly. If you can see the target clearly you can't see the sights. But that's what a lot of guys do— they look at the target so hard their sights blur and they don't hit. So, remember, look at the *sights.*"

Adam took the rifle and aimed at the pressure dial of the torpedo tube.

Jason sat on the wet steel deck and observed him. Then he took the rifle back. "I guess I'd better show you the four positions. Standing, kneeling, sitting and prone. With the sling."

"Now, Jason," the southerner said, "tell me the truth now. Did you *evah* see any marine at all in the line shootin' from any of those positions? And did you evah see any marine use his sling for anything but to tote that gun with?"

"I never did," Jason admitted, "but they made me learn all those positions."

"Don't inflict the lieutenant with all that. Just teach him to make that gun part of his hand. Part of *him.* Because I don't think wheah we're going is going to be healthy. At *all*."

The whole business still seemed unreal to Adam. Squatting in this submarine with a bunch of, by now, bad-smelling marines learning how to shoot a rifle. He kept asking himself, "What am *I* doing here?" And there seemed to be no answer.

He was yawning now and even Jason was beginning to drift off. But by this time Adam knew why and knew, with dread, that there were going to be some hours now which were going to seem absolutely endless. He was going to live through an eternity of misery in the next few hours. He wondered if the marines who just passed out weren't luckier than he was?

The submarine was now far into the territory of the enemy and, without its torpedoes, it was a helpless thing. It could not risk being seen by the enemy and so, at dawn of each day, it would submerge and stay submerged through the long, bright day, coming up only after the sun was well down and the night dark.

The only other navy man the marines had any real contact with was an old chief torpedoman who thought the torpedo room was his personal kingdom. At first he blamed the marines for the foul air. "There's supposed to be seventy people breathing this air and there's air enough for *them*. Then you phony heroes come in here and make it ninety-two men all gulping the same air and fouling it up."

But, as each day was the same, the chief finally admitted that something was haywire with the auxiliary air system and, until they fixed it, it was going to be rugged. (They never got it fixed.) The marines found out the first day that the chief had stuff that could absorb the carbon dioxide that was making them sick. They were little cakes, like soap, which he could spread around. But getting him to break them out and use them was almost useless. "These are for emergencies," he told them.

"What you think this is?" the southerner demanded. "Ah'm dyin' an' that's an emergency."

"Die," the chief said, "it'll be good for you."

The hours under the water were torture. By noon you had a headache of such intensity that the pain disarranged everything you did. And as the oxygen grew more scarce, there wasn't much you could do. By midafternoon the marines had stopped almost all movement. The talking died out, the card playing drifted to a stop, reading or writing became too painful to endure. There was nothing they could do but stand, or sit, or squat or, for the lucky ones, lie down in the bunks or torpedo racks or on the deck.

Orderly thought gave way then to the fear which began in the late afternoon and kept building up, hour after hour.

"Atmosphere."

Adam had never thought about it before. Atmosphere. It was just something that was always there, all around you. All around the whole world. Everybody had atmosphere so you didn't have to think about it.

But now, in these afternoons, the marines thought about it.

The chief torpedoman had told them about "atmosphere." "Atmosphere," the chief had said, "is just air. But in a submarine atmosphere is all the air there is in the boat. When we submerge we take aboard as much air as we can and that, friend, is all there is, there ain't no more. Now you Gyrenes keep horsing around and telling all these stories about how you're heroes and that uses up the atmosphere."

"Where do hit *go?*" the southerner asked him.

"It goes into CO_2," the chief told him. "Carbon dioxide. The same stuff that puts out fires—and it'll put you out, too. Now you take ordinary atmosphere, the stuff you breathe outside, that's only got three hundredths of *one* per cent of carbon dioxide. But by the time you Gyrenes get through telling everybody how great you are the CO_2 count goes way up—maybe two, two and a half per cent."

"How far can it go?" Adam asked him.

"Now, that I don't know," the chief said. "All the way, I guess, but the important thing is how far can *you* go. Some guys I know pass out when the CO_2 count goes above two point five. Some can stand it as high as two point eight. But nobody can stay conscious when it hits three and at four per cent you're dead."

So that became a sort of grisly game—listening to the occasional reports which came in to the marines through the loudspeaker on the bulkhead. Somebody would give an order: "Test atmosphere." Then the marines would wait, all of them staring at the loudspeaker, until the loudspeaker would answer. "Atmosphere reads carbon dioxide one point eight . . ." or nine or, once, two per cent.

By sundown the air would become so foul that, to Adam, the light bulbs seemed to be burning inside a gray, thick fog. Some of the marines would pass out on the deck and there was nothing you could do for them—they only needed air and there wasn't any more. Their faces, Adam noticed, gradually turned from a pink flesh color to a dull, light gray and, by nightfall, blue. No one smoked because there wasn't enough oxygen to keep a flame burning.

Adam had never realized before how blessed air could be. Just the opening of a small round steel door became, to the marines, the greatest event in their lives. It was something they looked forward to hour after hour; something they waited for with all their minds and bodies; something they prayed would happen—and happen soon. As the days went on, the miserable and endless days, three words got to be more important to them than any they had ever waited for.

Adam became convinced that every marine in the boat would rather hear those three words than, say, "Here's a million dollars."

They waited all day to hear them, and some, overcome by the lack of oxygen, never did hear them and the last hour of waiting always felt as though it could not be endured but, at last, a voice would say, "Open the hatch."

Then the air would pour down on them. Sweet, cool, fresh air—all you wanted of it. Tasting and smelling of the open ocean. Good, clean, fine *air*. At the order to open up, the marines—those who could move—would crowd in under the hatch, their faces upraised and waiting for the first inrush of the air. It made no difference to them if it was pouring rain or if the sea was rough and salt water spattered down on them, they kept their faces up to gulp in the fine air.

But, each day, until the air gave out Jason spent the hours trying to make a combat marine of Adam.

"Remember, Lieutenant," Jason began, "your feet are the most important part of you. Keep 'em clean and keep clean socks on 'em and see that your shoes fit. A lot of guys get killed because their feet get so sore and rotten they can't run fast enough."

"I'll do that," Adam said. It was a night, the pumps were circulating the good air through the boat and he and Jason, had, for a change, a little room. Most of the marines were up on the after platform of the sub, crowded together in the small place but at least able to look up at the stars and the moon and clouds, and look around without seeing a steel wall. "Listen, Jason," Adam said, "how about knocking off the 'lieutenant' stuff. That's for parades and I don't think we're going to be parading much. My first name's Adam. What's yours?"

"I'd rather just be called Jason," Jason said. "My first name's Harold."

"I don't much blame you."

"You know, I was telling you about the first-aid kit," Jason said, and Adam wondered why his voice suddenly sounded a little timid, shy. "Remember, if somebody gets hit, don't use your own kit on him. Use *his*. That way, when you get hit your buddy will have yours to use on you. That's important." He stopped for a moment and then said, quietly, "That is, if you *have* a buddy."

"That guy—what was his name, Rivers?—meant a lot to you, didn't he?" Adam asked.

"Brooks was his name," Jason said and then looked over at the torpedo tube. "Well, he was my buddy. You've *got* to have a buddy. They taught us that in boot camp and they were right. Without a buddy you're nothing. You're all by yourself. It's like this," Jason said, turning back to Adam, "one man can only do what one man can do, but—and I don't know why it is—two men can do as much as four or five. I don't know why that is. You just get a lot more fighting done with a buddy."

Adam had no intention of doing any fighting at all. He hadn't joined up to do this personal kind of fighting; this hand-to-hand stuff Jason had been trying to teach him. It wasn't that Adam was afraid of getting killed or anything like that. Your chances of living in a plane were no better than those of a man on the ground. But in a plane it was an impersonal thing—it was the *plane. That* did the fighting, you just drove it. Adam really couldn't imagine what it was like to fight on the ground, one man against another.

"What was it like on Guadalcanal?" he asked.

"Oh, I don't know," Jason said. "I guess I had the wrong idea. You know, going to the movies and all. It wasn't much like that. You know these guys in the movies get hit and this pretty girl comes out of nowhere and takes care of him and all that." Jason began to laugh. "And they're so clean—

in the movies. Oh, maybe they've got a couple smudges of mud way up on their cheekbones or something. On Guadal you weren't ever clean. I mean, your clothes were rotting off you and you were rotting inside them. We were *dirty*. I don't know, it seems like they always arrange it so you're about as uncomfortable as you can get. Like this." He waved his hand around at the steel walls.

Adam remembered the beak-nosed marine talking to him one night on the after platform. "That Jason is a real marine," Guns had told him. "He's one marine who ought to have all the medals they've got. And just a kid."

"What'd he do?" Adam had asked.

"Nothing," Guns had said. "He didn't go running around killing off thousands of people and being a nuisance. He was just always where he was supposed to be and you could count on him to stay there. No matter how bad it got Jason would stay there. Nothing could shake him. I remember once they came pouring down on him—I tell you it looked like a *million* of 'em. I would've run a country mile. But Jason stayed." Guns stopped and thought a minute. "The way he's smart is like that time. He figured that even these guys weren't attacking marines for the glory of the Emperor, or whatever. Somebody was telling 'em to, just like somebody was always telling us; somebody was leading 'em. So he sat there in a mudhole and picked off the ones he thought were the boss. He must've been right because, after a while, they stopped coming and went on back where they'd come from. He's a good man in a fire fight," Guns decided. "A real marine."

2 Three things were constantly in the minds of the marines as the long voyage went on: the air, the submarine and, finally, the destination. As they got used to the terrible air of the days and the sweet air of the nights; and learned to endure the unendurable crowding and inconvenience (not one of them had had any sort of bath for four days unless the sweat that poured from them in the 100-degree heat could be called a bath) the destination began to emerge as the most important of the three things.

Each marine had his own idea of where they were going and what they were going to do when they got there. (One of them insisted that they were going back to the States, although the compass above the torpedo tubes held steadily on a course which, unless they went around the world, would never bring this submarine to the States.)

"I figure it this way," Jason told Adam. "It's going to be a jungle someplace."

"What do we need with a jungle?"

"Well, it could come in handy," Jason said vaguely, not sure what we needed with one. "But it's going to be a jungle because we're the only marines who ever fought 'em in a jungle. They've got lots of parade-ground marines and recruiting marines in their striped pants but we're all—except you, that is—First Regiment, First Division Marines. We're the first to have a stand-up fight with 'em. And we licked 'em. They're supposed to be red-hot in this jungle fighting and I guess they are. Anyway, we licked 'em at the Tenaru. You know how to get their snipers out of the palm trees?"

"Remember, Jason, I'm no warrior."

"You will be. Anyway, you get a light tank and butt it against the trunks of the trees. The snipers fall out like coconuts and away we go. So, anyway, I figure we're going to some jungle."

"We're going to Australia. We're going to do sentry duty on those kangaroos."

"We're going back to the Philippines," the tech sergeant

said. "MacArthur left his hat. So we're going to go back and get it."

"I think this is some kind of endurance test," one of them decided. "They put us on Guadalcanal and that couldn't kill us so somebody in Washington got to wondering what *could* kill us and so they decided to see if we could *wear* out. We're just going to ride around and around inside this iron cigar until we wear out."

The staff sergeant spoke with authority. "It's a mission. It's a combat mission or they wouldn't have picked us. And, wherever we're going, it's going to be hot or we wouldn't be wearing these thin fatigues."

"Are we all there are?" one of them asked plaintively. "Just twenty of us—not counting you, Lieutenant? Maybe the whole regiment, maybe the division is coming along. Maybe all the Navy's subs have got marines in 'em."

"I don't think so," the sergeant said. "They picked us out, two by two, from all over the division. Special Weapons men, R-2 people, gunnery sergeants, Com-Section men, with fire teams and BAR men. That doesn't look like a big action to me. If they'd wanted a big action, they'd have said, 'Fall in, March Off!'"

"I don't think we're going to fight," another declared. "They're going to dump us on some barren rock as an occupation force and let us sit there with the gooney birds."

"I don't want to confuse everybody," Adam put in, "but it looks to me like I foul up everybody's theory. If we're an assault team—why me? I never assaulted anything. If we're going to occupy an island—why me? They paid about fifty thousand dollars to teach me to be a pilot. Why throw all that—and me—away?"

The tech sergeant looked at him for a moment and asked, sarcastically, "What *can* you do, Lieutenant?"

"I drive plane pretty good," Adam said, not boasting.

All the marines looked at him then and it gave Adam a funny feeling. They didn't look at him with scorn or even with superiority. They looked at him as you would a Christmas present from your little old aunt; a prettily wrapped gismo that was perfectly useless to you. Adam felt strongly that he was out of place here. Even, perhaps, unwanted.

"The reason they didn't tell us where we're going," Guns said, "is because we don't want to know."

"No you don't, Rebel," Guns said. "If they take you prisoner and start working you over the less you know the better your chances of coming out of it. If they think you know something and won't tell 'em—then . . . well, you're in for a real going over and they know how to go over you too."

Jason said it for all of them. "I don't much care where we go, just get me out of *here*. I'd rather be nailed down on some stinking beach than live in this coffin."

On the fourth night, soon after the hatches were opened and the air poured in, word came over the speaker for all marines to report to the forward torpedo room.

Adam and Jason, with four or five others, were taking their turn on the after part of the open bridge and hated to leave before their hour of the night sky, the rushing white sea, and the stars and the air was over but, as one of them said, "This must be it."

In the torpedo room the colonel and the major were waiting as Adam and the rest shoved their way into the already packed room.

As the marines settled down, Jason whispered to Adam, "That's the colonel who led the Scouts on Guadalcanal. Real rugged."

"They had *Boy Scouts* on Guadalcanal?" Adam asked in a loud whisper.

Jason looked at him with scorn. "Yeh. Boy Scouts. About nine feet tall."

"With merit badges?"

"With merit badges. Like the Purple Heart and Medal of Honor. That's one you don't usually get until after you're dead."

"Who needs it?" Adam said.

Across the room the colonel and the major were setting up big photographs and charts on the torpedo tubes. Looking over the heads of the others Adam could see pictures of dark islands in an almost perfect circle. They were like a necklace with many small islands making a chain from which hung one big island, much darker than the rest.

Adam decided that the colonel was neither very polite nor very considerate. He made no apology for not telling them long ago what this trip was all about. He just started talking, saying, "I haven't told you men where you are going or what you are going to do because it wasn't necessary for you to know. Until now." He swung around to the pictures. "This is where you're going. It's an atoll whose real name it is not important for you to know. It is held by the enemy. Only one of the islands—this one"—he pointed to the big dark pendant in the necklace—"concerns us, for that's where the enemy is. We're going ashore there."

To Adam the marines seemed only glad to hear the news. Glad, he supposed, because it meant getting out of this steel coffin. But, he wondered, did they—or even the colonel— realize that there might be *thousands* of the enemy on that island? What could a couple of dozen marines accomplish against odds like that?

This was a real nightmare. Somebody, somewhere, was fouling things up beyond belief.

The colonel was talking. "This is going to be a recon. We want to find out whether the enemy has built an airfield here. If so, what is it made of—crushed coral? Concrete? What? How long is it? How wide? Taxi strips? Revetments?

Hangars? Repair facilities? And, above all, the number and types of aircraft on the island, if any? Also, what will it take to put the strip out of commission—the size and type of bombs or shells.

"Next we've got to find out what sort of fortifications they've got, what we'll have to fight if, later, we attack this place. Pillboxes? Where? How many? Above or below the ground? What are they made of? What's the best way to knock them out? Bombing from the air? Fire from surface ships? Or do the Marines have to take them with rifles and flame? What's in the pillboxes? Machine guns? Big? Little? AA? Shore batteries?

"Next, we want to find out the strength of the enemy. How many? What sort of troops? Army? Marine? Navy? How experienced? What training? How armed?

"Next is terrain. What sort of place is it for fighting? Hills? Thick jungle or open jungle? Sniper positions? Concealed artillery?

"In short," the colonel said, "we're going to find out everything there is to know about the enemy on this place. Any questions?"

The southerner looked around at his buddies for a moment, but since none of them had courage enough to ask he raised his hand. "Yes, sir, I have a question, Colonel."

Adam was surprised that there was now no trace of Rebel's southern accent. He sounded as though he came from Boston, Massachusetts.

"What is it, Stiles?"

"How do we get home again?" Rebel asked.

"The major will give you the details," the colonel said. Then he stopped talking and slowly looked at the marines, one by one. When he began talking again his voice was lower and the words came out slow and clear. "All of you were on Guadalcanal. All of you except Lieutenant Land.

"I told you; this is a recon. We are going to land on this island, get the information we want and get off the island. Obviously, if the enemy sees us coming, we won't get ashore. If we get ashore and the enemy finds us, we won't get off the island. Understand?"

Adam understood the words all right, but, from the looks on the faces of the marines around him, he began to wonder if he really understood the significance. The marines seemed to be sharing some sort of secret among themselves and he wondered what it was.

The colonel was looking at them again with that slow, steady gaze, his eyes looking into each man's eyes in turn. "The first shot you fire will kill us all," he said. "All right, Major, take over."

The men silently made a passage for the colonel and, as he approached, Adam stepped aside for him, but the colonel said, "Come with me, Lieutenant."

Adam followed him out of the torpedo room and down to the little cabin, where the colonel let him in and then closed the door.

"What sort of trip has it been?" the colonel asked.

"Well, lousy, sir."

The colonel smiled then and said, "I wonder if when we get through this war all we'll really remember about it is how uncomfortable it was." Now he turned again and smiled at Adam. "I'm sorry I couldn't explain all this to you back in Pearl, Land."

"I wish I knew more about this sort of thing," Adam said.

"Don't worry," the colonel said pleasantly, "those marines are hand-picked, they know their job. You just go along with them."

"Colonel, why am I here at all?" Adam asked.

"Those IBM machines in Washington are pretty efficient," the colonel said. "I needed an aviator who could judge the

air strength and facilities on the island. I also needed someone who could read and speak Japanese. The machine
picked you because you had lived and gone to school in Japan. You were also a naval aviator. You were also available
in Pearl Harbor. And expendable."

Adam thought to himself, this is the end of the dream.
Then he began to wonder what the real nightmare was going
to be like.

"That *is* you, isn't it?" the colonel asked. "Your father was
a professor at the University in Tokyo, wasn't he? You lived
there for four years, didn't you?"

Adam looked at him. "That's me, sir. And I guess I'm expendable."

"Just a phrase," the colonel said with a hint of apology.
"Now," he went on, "to spot the enemy armament, I needed
a detail for intelligence. I want you to go at this thing as
though you were going to command the air attack against
this island. Find out what resistance you can expect at the
beginning and then find out what facilities you will have
for your own use when the island is ours. Try, too, to get
any code books you can find or anything else that may help
us. I will probably go along with, or near, you, because their
air power is the most important thing we want to find out."

"When do we go, Colonel?"

"Tomorrow night. We will be in the vicinity of the atoll
tomorrow afternoon. We'll find out as much as we can
through the periscope and then we'll make sure the entrance to the lagoon isn't mined. At nightfall we'll go into
the lagoon, submerged, then surface and we'll go ashore in
the rubber boats. We'll only have eight hours, Lieutenant.
We've got to be off the island before dawn."

"The sub's coming back for us?"

"It'll wait in the lagoon, then surface before dawn and
pick us up. Get a good night's sleep."

"I'll try," Adam said, grinning.

When he got back to the torpedo room the major had gone but the pictures and the charts were still there.

Adam had expected that the marines would be yakking up a storm about all this. It was what he wanted to do. Just to hear them talk about it, he thought, would made the thing less enormous, maybe. Make it less terrifying.

But the marines were very quiet. Most of them were fooling with their rifles—*again*. Taking them apart, inspecting every inch of every piece, then putting them carefully back together again. Then cleaning them—rifles so clean already that it seemed impossible to get them any cleaner.

Adam found Jason sitting on one of the bunks—cleaning his rifle—and squeezed in beside him. "Well," Adam said, hoping that Jason would talk about it.

"Yeh," Jason said, inspecting his rifle. "Well."

"Big night tomorrow night, eh?"

"Could be," Jason admitted.

He didn't seem to want to talk at all. Adam watched him clean the rifle for a long time and, as he sat there, he began to feel really scared and, more than that even, lonely. "Suppose the place is crawling with Japs?" Adam asked.

"Probably is," Jason said, swinging his rifle up so he could sight through the barrel at the overhead light. "Hmmm," he said and began to clean the barrel again.

After a while Adam asked, "What do you think about the whole deal, Jason?"

"Nothing," Jason said.

Jason just wasn't interested in anything.

"What did the major say?" Adam asked.

"Same old stuff," Jason said.

"Anything I ought to know, perhaps?"

"Unh unh," Jason said, taking his ammo clips out of their

pouches and lightly oiling each round before putting them back.

Adam looked slowly around the crowded room and it seemed to him then that each marine had, somehow, walled himself off from all the others; each becoming as alone as the last man on earth.

"At least I found out why I'm here," Adam said.

Jason, he could tell, wasn't interested but at least he was polite as he said, "Yeah? Why?"

"I speak Japanese."

Jason turned slowly and, at last, looked at him. "You speak Japanese?"

"Yeah. I lived in Japan for four or five years. My old man was a professor in the University in Tokyo."

"Yeh? And you speak it real good?"

"I ought to. It's all I spoke for four or five years. My father wanted us to, so we even spoke it to each other."

Jason carefully put his rifle down where it wouldn't get dirty and then said, "Hey, you guys!"

The marines turned to look at him.

"Get this," Jason said. "Adam speaks Japanese. He speaks it good!"

The marines looked then at Adam with interest. The Rebel said, "You really speak that language?"

"I speak it better than you do dat ol' southern drawl," Adam told him. "How come when you talk to the colonel you sound like you went to Harvard or something?"

"Sssh," the Rebel said. "Ah'm keepin' the colonel off balance so he won't find out ah'm a general in the Confederate Army." Suddenly the Rebel cut loose with a bloodcurdling yell and then looked around at all of them. "Look out, you Yankees, *you*," he said. "The South shall rise again."

"Amen, brother," Guns said and turned to Adam. "You really speak it, huh? Well, let me tell you, it may save your little ol' life, it may. I lost my whole squad one time because none of us could speak the language. This patrol came by where we were and I guess they suspected we were around there because they kept hollering that old 'Marine, you die!' stuff. So when they really got us in a tight, I was wishing, boy, I could speak that language. I'd've said, like the meanest DI in the Corps, 'Stop making so much noise or the Marines will *kill* you.' But, of course, I couldn't say a word and they found us."

"Ah know one thing for sho'," the Rebel said. "Ah'm gonna go along with Adam heah so if we git in a little trouble Adam can say to 'em in their own language, 'Ain't nobody heah but us chickens, boss,' and they'll go away."

"All right, you guys," Guns said, "get some sleep. Douse the light somebody."

As the bright lights went out and left the room lit only by the red battle light Adam watched the marines bedding down. The speaking-the-language thing had brought him a little closer to them but now as they tried to find some comfortable position for sleep they seemed to him to be men from Mars, or somewhere. How could they—with the map of that island lit now with a reddish glow—just go to sleep like this?

It was his turn for the deck, with Jason in the bunk above it and as Adam stretched out on the cool steel and arranged his helmet for a pillow he felt everything starting to become real, as though he were waking up from a dream to find that it had not, really, been a dream at all.

Adam looked at the photographs of the atoll—the pretty, palm-covered little islands surrounding their deep and calm lagoon and, slowly, the photographs became real—the coral and sand and trees and surf were real.

But he, himself, did not yet feel real. They had asked (asked?) him to go ashore on that island. To go ashore, practically alone, on that enemy-held island. To go ashore, and inspect the enemy's defenses, his airstrip and planes and hangars, his shops and spare parts.

Adam, lying on the deck, was appalled. This was so far beyond anything he had ever imagined that he could not now grasp it in his mind. He could not see himself doing this thing. Sometimes, while sitting on his surfboard waiting for a good set to start moving in, he had imagined himself as a dashing navy hero, his chest covered with medals. He would have a slight, but attractive-type, wound somewhere. But this heroic Adam Land, of the United States Navy, had done his feats of valor in the clean blue sky while flying an airplane in a very dashing manner. He had never imagined himself in a situation like this.

It scared the daylights out of him. Really terrified him and he suddenly wished that he could just vanish. Disappear. Then, after a while, there would be Adam Land lying on some California beach, his surfboard, skeg up, lying on the sand beside him and with nothing in the world to do but wait for the surf to begin to move.

He did not, somehow, vanish.

3   In the conning tower the marine colonel stood out of the way in the crowded little room with its busy people. The skipper and executive officer were there, the helmsman, the soundman, the talker, the chief of the boat, a quartermaster and the first lieutenant.

In the center of the rectangular room there was a round hole in the deck and up through this hole the oiled steel shaft of the periscope went straight up and through the ceiling. The skipper walked over to it now and said, "Up periscope."

Motors somewhere in the bowels of the ship began to hum

and the skipper stooped down and held his hands out as though warming them at a fire. The oily shaft started moving slowly up, then gathered speed and, in a moment, the base of the scope appeared. Two handles, much like the handlebars of a motorcycle, were folded up against the scope shaft and the skipper took them now and flipped them down so that they stuck out perpendicular to the shaft. With these handles he could not only turn the scope around the horizon, he could focus it and make other adjustments.

Stooping a little, with his face against a rubber guard around the eyepiece he swung the scope slowly around. Finally he stopped turning it and stood still for a moment, his face against the rubber shield. Then he stepped away from the scope and said to the other officer, "Well done, Jonesy. Right on the money." The skipper then turned to the colonel. "Here's your island, Colonel."

The colonel came over to the scope and looked for a long time through the eyepiece.

The submarine was on the seaward and windward side of the atoll, so the colonel could see almost nothing of the place where, in a few hours, he would have to land marines. A heavy and continuous surf was breaking on the coral reef between the submarine and the island and the spray from this surf made a solid curtain of white water. Through this curtain the colonel could see nothing, and over it all he could see was the tops of the palm trees and, from periscope height, even these looked unreal and hazy.

"Aren't you in rather close?" the colonel asked, still looking through the scope.

"We're in a hundred fathoms of water," the skipper said, unworried.

"I was thinking of mines," the colonel said.

"I doubt if they would put mines on the seaward side," the skipper said. "They know, as well as you do, that the only way to attack an island such as this is from the lagoon side. Mining this side would just be a waste."

"That's the logical way to look at it," the colonel agreed, stepping back from the scope, "but marine corps doctrine holds that if the only way to attack an enemy position is at Point A—in this case the lagoon side—then attack him at any other point."

"Have you ever seen the surf breaking against these islands, Colonel?" the skipper asked and then ordered, "Down scope."

"No, I haven't," the colonel admitted.

"Unbelievable," the skipper said. "The waves breaking here now have been coming for a thousand, two thousand miles. Nothing in the deep sea has hindered them so you don't think of the pressure in them. But when they hit one of these little atolls . . . well, it's noisy. They are just tremendous waves. Nothing could live through them." He turned to the colonel. "So I doubt if they would mine this area. On the other hand, they may have mined the lagoon entrance."

"What can you do about that?" the colonel asked.

"Their mine fields aren't very effective. At least, so far in the war. Too few and too shallow. We usually just dive under 'em."

"How far are we from the lagoon entrance?" the colonel asked.

The skipper glanced at his chart. "We're exactly on schedule, colonel. Thirty-five miles from the lagoon entrance. We'll go into the lagoon at eighteen hundred, just after sunset."

The colonel looked at the clock on the wall. "It's going to be a long seven hours," he said.

"The next eight are going to be longer, aren't they?" the skipper asked.

"Waiting is worse than fighting," the colonel said, and added, "Pass the word for B squad to meet me in the wardroom."

4　　In the forward torpedo room the marines were pretty sure what was going on although they could not hear the conversation in the conning tower. But this was D day and B squad had been called aft to the wardroom, so there was nothing to do now but wait.

That morning each of them had been issued one helmet full of water and now all of them had shaved for the first time since coming aboard the boat. Then, with the soapy shaving water left, they had washed themselves as well as they could. To Adam they looked a lot cleaner and smelled a lot better than they had before.

The torpedo room had changed also. The chaos Adam had grown used to—the gear all over the place, the sweat-soaked clothes hanging anywhere to dry a little, the marines sprawling, wherever they could find space—was gone. Now each man's combat gear was packed and neatly stacked around the walls of the room. The rifles were ready, and each had an oil-soaked rag stuck in the muzzle, other rags protecting the sights and action. The bayonets had been honed during the long days to razor edges and needle points and were now in their oiled scabbards. Adam could see a possible use for the bayonets but since they had been given strict orders not to fire under any circumstances he wondered what good it would do to carry the rifles.

There was tension among them now—the first real tension Adam had seen. Up until now these marines had treated the whole thing as a routine operation; just another skirmish. Now, though, they were tense, each a little withdrawn. The usual loud laughter and constant griping and minor arguments were all gone. The ones who had not gone aft now sat around the torpedo room quietly talking or just staring at nothing.

For some reason they were talking about the Marine Corps itself. The chief torpedoman had gotten them started on that subject by making some sarcastic remark about marines and they were still yakking about it.

The chief was old—maybe thirty or forty years old, and grouchy. He tried his best to ignore them. He acted as though they did not really exist as he moved about in his kingdom below the sea and the marines had learned to get out of his way because he thought nothing of stepping on your face or anywhere else his foot decided to come down.

The chief blamed the marines for everything—the lack of torpedoes, the weak condition of the batteries, the breakdown of the auxiliary air system.

Today, however, the chief was in a good humor. He came into the torpedo room with a wan smile which vanished when he found that the after door had been left open. He yelled something about the watertight integrity of the ship as he swung the heavy steel door shut and swung all the handles around, clamping the door into the frame. Then he stalked over to his throne—a little platform between the torpedo tubes—got up on it and looked at Adam and the nine marines with a cold, disapproving eye. "The happiest day of my life," the chief announced. "In five more hours you punks will be out of my torpedo room."

"And in thirteen more we'll be right back," Adam reminded him.

That depressed the chief until he had a happy thought. "Maybe the Japs will eat you alive," he hoped. "Or maybe I can talk the skipper into going on home without waiting for you punks to show up."

"Now, chiefy," Adam said, "you wouldn't leave us all-

American boys stranded out here in enemy territory, would you?"

"I'd be delighted," the chief said. Then he looked at them again. "You don't look like warriors to me," he decided.

They didn't look like warriors to Adam either. They were half naked and sweating in the heat, barefooted, and all the tan long gone, so that they were pale white. Even the lean, mean look was fading.

"How do they *make* marines?" the chief wanted to know. "You guys look like anybody else, you act like anybody else, only worse. You come from the same places everybody else does. So what do they do to you to give you the idea that you're *somebody?* That you're some sort of heroes? That you're gonna win 'em all and never lose one."

"What does 'lose' mean, chiefy?" one of the marines asked.

"That's what I *mean?*" the chief yelled at him. "You all think you're Superman, or something. What do they do to you in boot camp, sit you down twenty-four hours a day and brainwash you into thinking you're *great*. Do they make you say a thousand times a day, 'I am a marine. I am the greatest thing on two legs?' What do they do to you in boot camp so you come out different from everybody else?"

Adam decided that the only reason the marines now took the chief seriously was because of the time. In a few more hours they'd be in the rubber boats on their way toward the hostile island. It was therefore a time for seriousness— or silliness. And they were serious.

They looked at each other after the chief asked them that and one of them said, "I don't know about you guys, but in boot camp I don't remember them telling me anything about being a marine. Just *be* one or get your head busted."

"They sho' nevah tol' me Ah was no Superman," Rebel

said. "Just the opposite. Ah thought Ah was doin' real good
if they thought Ah was a livin' human bein'."

"Yeh," another agreed. "It didn't seem to me that you
were *anybody*. You were just part of the Marine Corps, the
whole shebang."

"The only time you were anybody was if you let the Corps
down. *Then* you were somebody—in the guardhouse on
bread and water."

"I think that was it," Guns said. "That all-for-one and
one-for-all. That finally got through to me."

"I don't know," another one said, thinking it over. "I used
to wonder about the Marine Corps. I used to wonder what
a marine really was. Then I saw one. You remember Bloody
Ridge, Rebel?"

"It was named for me," Rebel said.

"They said, 'Hold your fire or you'll give away your position.' Well, I saw a marine hold his fire until they walked
up and shot him. But because he did, we wiped 'em *out*."

Jason, who was sitting next to Adam on the deck, said,
not to the room but only to Adam, "I guess the first time
I understood anything about being a marine was in boot
camp. You remember in boot camp you had those field-gear
inspections?"

Adam was almost ashamed to admit that he had never
been in a boot camp. To hear these marines tell it, if you
hadn't been to boot camp you'd never make it as a marine,
or anything else. "I didn't go to boot camp. Remember?"
Adam said, "I guess they figured it was too rugged for me."

"Maybe because you were an officer," Jason decided.
"Anyway, in boot camp we had this DI. That's a drill instructor. I'll never forget that guy. When you first join up
I don't know what you think but whatever it is you don't
think your life is going to spin down to just one guy. But
it does. That DI gets to be the biggest thing there *is*. You

just can't believe that any one man can get so important. It was funny," Jason decided thinking about it. "I wasn't scared of this DI as a *person*. In fact, I sort of liked him as a person. I was scared because if you goofed up you knew it wouldn't be any trouble at all for this DI to go out and get a bolt of lightning and drive it right through your head. But he wouldn't do it just because you aggravated *him;* he'd do it because you'd goofed up in the *Marine Corps*.

"Anyway, there was a fellow in my platoon who was, I think, just plain nuts. He couldn't get with it at all. He was a real quiet, thin guy; real serious. And he tried. I mean he didn't fight it, he just couldn't get with it. No matter what he did it was wrong. Now you'd think that DI would give him a hard time—a harder time than he gave the rest of us, and that was about as hard a time as you could find— but he didn't. He kept working with this fellow trying to get him with it.

"So, one day, we were having this inspection. You know, you take all your gear—the whole works—and lay it out for the DI to inspect. There's only one way to lay it out and that's the marine corps way. No other way. So the DI came along and when he got to this fellow's gear the fellow had his bayonet lying the wrong way. So the DI said, 'Jenkins,'— that was this fellow's name—'your bayonet should be lying this way.' So Jenkins picked up the bayonet but, instead of laying it down the way it should be, he swung around with that bayonet and drove it right through the DI's leg, up above the knee. All the way through so we could see half that bayonet sticking out the other side of the DI's leg.

"Well," Jason said, still wondering about it, "the rest of us thought '*Look out!*' We thought the roof was going to fall on him and the ground open up and swallow him and there was going to be lightning and thunder and this fellow Jenkins would wind up obliterated. Because you just don't pick up a bayonet and ram it through a DI's leg. You don't do that.

"You know what that DI did?" Jason asked, but before Adam could answer, he said, "Nothing. That DI didn't do *anything*. It's hard to believe it, even for me who saw him, but he just stood there without even changing his expression. He didn't show any pain, any surprise, any anger. *Nothing!* After a while he reached down and pulled the bayonet out of his leg. And then you know what he did? He wiped the bayonet off and put it down the way it was supposed to be in the first place and then he straightened up and said to this Jenkins—he said it just like he said everything—he said, 'Jenkins, you and I had better go see the doctor.' We never saw that Jenkins again. I guess the headshrinkers figured out he was a nut or something. But, next day, that DI was back with us and he never said a word about it. He was the first real marine I ever saw," Jason said.

"The most dangerous weapon in the world is a United States marine with his rifle," one of them said, in a loud voice and then broke up laughing.

It started them all laughing and they were laughing and yakking when, all of a sudden, the chief's voice came down on them like thunder. *"Silence!"*

It was so loud, so commanding and so unexpected that, for a second, the marines went along with it, then Rebel said, "Now, chiefy, what's ailin' you?"

The chief swung around on him and said, *"Shut up!"*

This time they all knew that he meant it and they were silent as they sat there, looking at the chief for some explanation.

The chief was standing in the middle of the torpedo room, leaning a little to his right. His eyes were closed, his mouth a little open, his body motionless. Then, without opening his eyes, he walked on tiptoe a few paces and stopped.

Now the marines heard the sound the chief had heard.

Ordinarily there were a great many sounds in the torpedo room. Even submerged, with the electric motors running, there were sounds. Sounds of the motors and auxiliaries, sounds of people working, or changing the watch; commands, conversation, music; the sounds of cooking in the galley, of cleaning up. A great many sounds, all blending finally into a steady level of sound which, in a little while, you no longer heard.

When the boat was on the surface at night there were more and different sounds. The diesels made a heavy, throbbing sound and the sea itself made sounds—the waves crashing against the bow of the boat could be clearly heard inside the torpedo room and, if it rained, that could be heard tattooing on the deck above their heads.

However, when the boat was submerged there was no sound at all from the outside world. No sound at all came from the water around them.

So, now, this sound coming from outside the boat was so unusual that it was frightening.

To Adam it sounded as though someone outside the boat, in the sea, was scraping the steel hull of the submarine with something else made of metal. It was a clear, close sound, not very loud; not with any force, just a metallic scraping.

The chief yanked the phone out of its cradle on the wall and yelled, "Con! Con! Something's touching the boat. Starboard side, forward. Sounds like metal."

The reaction in the conning tower was instantaneous, the voice of the skipper saying, "Stop all engines! . . . All back, one third . . . All stop."

Adam who, with the marines, had unconsciously gotten up on his feet stood now staring at the loudspeaker. As the boat came to a stop in the water the sound also stopped.

"I don't hear it," the chief said into the phone.

The skipper's voice now came over the loudspeaker. "Give me a reading, sound."

"A hundred fathoms, sir."

"Quiet in the boat!" the skipper said. "Shut down everything."

All the familiar sounds began to disappear. The hum of the electric motors stopped, the little whines of the auxiliaries dropped in pitch and stopped. The sound of working, cooking, music—everything—stopped. It was the quietest place Adam had ever been in.

In the wardroom ten of the combat marines, the colonel and the major sat crowded together in motionless silence, their eyes, too, fixed on the loudspeaker which was now a silent metal grille set into the wall.

In the motor-control room the electricians' mates stood without moving, hardly breathing. In front of them a bank of three-foot-long, brass-handled levers which controlled the electric circuits of the motors shone oilily in the bright light. The hands of the men were poised near the levers, ready to move whenever the order came.

In the motor room the motormacs on duty stood near the switchboards, their eyes running nervously over the maze of wires and circuit breakers, gauges and dials.

In the crew's quarters, the engine room, the radio shack, the galley, the after torpedo room; in the officers' quarters and control room men stood, waiting, listening . . . silent.

In the conning tower the skipper, moving without a sound, got to the phone and said, almost whispering, "What do you hear, chief?"

In the forward torpedo room the chief's voice, also whispering, sounded, in that silence, almost loud and rasping, "I don't hear it now, sir."

"Now, hear this, all hands," the skipper said, his voice coming low and quiet through the loudspeakers. "Let's back her out of here. Very slowly. Straight back the way we came in. You men on the planes . . . keep her absolutely level. Helmsman, you hold her straight when she begins to move. Stand by to move her."

In the torpedo room Adam looked around at the chief and the marines and, for some reason, it reminded him of that tense, awful silence that came when you first saw your paper at a big exam in school and read the terrible questions they had asked you.

The skipper's voice came over, real low and steady, "Okay, all back. Just turn 'em over, mac. But keep 'em even."

The low humming of the electric motors began, breaking the deep silence in the boat. Adam could feel a slow, slow gentle backward movement begin.

And with the movement the sound of metal touching the boat on the outside began again, also.

Now the sound was a terrible thing to hear. An unknown and awful sound.

"It's touching us," the chief said into the phone.

There was no answer from con, no sound from the speaker.

Adam felt sweat running through his eyebrows and down into his eyes. He let it run, not moving anything except his eyelids, as the rasping, metallic sound continued.

Then, as suddenly as it had begun, it stopped. There was now no sound except the low hum of the motors.

"It's stopped," the chief said.

Then a faint voice came over the speaker, a voice not talking into the microphone—just talking. "I can't hold her, Skipper," the voice said, "the stern's swinging to starboard."

The chief said into the phone, "Whatever it is must be caught in the bow plane, Skipper. I don't hear anything now."

The faint voice said over the speaker, "It feels like she's caught in something."

The skipper's voice came loud and clear, "Rig in the starboard bow plane."

It was the last thing he said.

Adam listened to the sound of the bow plane motor as it slowed against the pressure of the big plane moving through the water. Then there was the sound inside the boat of the plane's hinges slowly closing, metal moving on metal.

The chief had explained to Adam how the bow planes worked. They were like the fins on a fish. Submerged, the planes were unfolded outward into the water, long, flat planes which you could turn on an axis to create pressure either on top or bottom of the plane's surface. This way they kept the boat moving level through the water.

On the surface, the bow planes were rigged in—folded back into slots in the hull of the submarine so that they did not break her streamlined form.

The starboard bow plane was moving now, folding back toward the hollowed-out place in the hull.

Adam was used to this sound and waited now for the watery *clunk* noise the plane would make when it moved into place and was locked there by some mechanism.

Instead of the *clunk* the next sound Adam heard was so huge and unexpected that it was not a sound at all. It was a *force*.

The deafening explosion jerked the room out from under them and then shook it violently. The last thing Adam saw before the lights went out was the torpedo room filled with floating bodies. Bodies of marines, sprawled out in the air, of rifles flying around, packs and canteens floating in space.

This is a Mickey Mouse, Adam thought, as he found that he, too, was afloat in the air. A cartoon where one character bops another character and the whole world explodes.

Lights, colors, whirligigs flash and spin. People go winging off into space, zooming away until they are only little dots. Vast holes appear in the ground and mountains collapse into rubble.

As he fell, the great sound around him subsided slowly so that he could hear a multitude of other sounds, none of them familiar.

It was now black-dark in the torpedo room. Adam struck something on his way down, bounced off it and struck again, this time the floor. He was trying to get up when someone else landed on him and smashed him back to the deck. Then other things rained down on him.

"Turn on the lights," Adam yelled, trying to get free of the body on top of him, but nothing happened.

Men were yelling and cursing; some of them were hurt. Adam got back on his feet and stumbled toward the emergency light switch near the door. But now the torpedo room was moving again, not as violently as before, but moving, tilting upward. The movement threw Adam down. He got up and went on, stepping on someone as he moved.

Above the sound of the men yelling for the lights, for each other, or just plain yelling, Adam could hear other sounds beyond the wall of the torpedo room but could not make them out.

The dim red emergency lights came on when he moved the switch. The torpedo room was wild. Half-naked marines were trying to get up, or stay up, their arms and legs waving around in the dim light. All their gear was moving around on the floor, rifles skidding along, packs rolling, canteens and helmets bouncing down toward Adam.

The deck of the torpedo room was dropping out from under them and the front end, where the tubes were, was rising.

As it rose the men could no longer keep their balance and
fell or rolled back down toward the wall.

Adam, already there, watched. Because he could see nothing beyond the room the only way he knew that it was tilting upward was the pull of gravity. As the front end went
on up Adam simply stepped out on the wall. Soon, from
the feel of it, Adam guessed that the submarine was now
hanging straight up and down in the water, the front end
straight up.

A marine was yelling, "We're going *down!* We're going
down." Nobody paid any attention to him until he started
fighting his way toward the door, pushing people aside,
throwing the gear around. "I'm getting outta here," he
yelled. "Get out of my way! Open the door!"

Guns caught him and pinned his arms. "Shape up or ship
out," he snapped. "Don't rush the situation."

Now the torpedo room began to turn slowly around. You
couldn't see it, but you could feel it—not a smooth turning;
rather a twisting, slow movement.

The marines who could get up were standing with Adam
on the wall. Others, hurt, were still lying in the tangle of
gear.

"Where's the chief?" Adam asked. "Chief!" he yelled.

But there was only the babble of voices. "What's happening?" "What hit us?" "We're sinking." "Do something!" And
one marine kept saying in a monotonous voice, "Where's my
rifle? Anybody seen my rifle?"

Adam tried to shut out the noise the marines were making hoping to hear again the old familiar sounds—the motors
whining, remote voices over the loudspeaker, the ordinary
faint sounds of the boat.

Instead he heard first a wet, steady, hissing sound coming from somewhere outside and below him. This kept up

while other sounds, metals grinding together, small, muffled explosions, creaking and banging came and went.

As the room continued to twist slowly around Adam noticed that the telephone was off the hook and was swinging back and forth on its cord, hitting against the torpedo tube, then bouncing away, to swing and whirl around.

Maybe somebody's trying to say something, Adam thought. Maybe I ought to answer it.

He started climbing up the deck toward the torpedo tubes above him. Jason said, "Where are you going, Adam?"

"To answer the phone," Adam told him, climbing up along the torpedo racks. Leaning out from the rack he caught the phone as it swung like a pendulum toward him. "Hello," he said. "Hello? Anybody there?"

There was no answer and the phone sounded dead. Then Adam felt stupid when he noticed the push-to-talk button. He pushed it down and said, "Hello? Hello?"

The phone still sounded dead. He shook it, listened, pushed the button. "Hello. Conning tower. Control? *Anybody!* This is the forward torpedo room. Do you read me? Do you read me?" He let the button up and listened. The phone was dead.

Adam was trying to hang it back in its cradle when he was suddenly and violently jerked loose from the torpedo rack and flung down. As he fell he could see the other men staggering and falling.

The noise around him as he fell was tremendous but not like the first great sound. This was slow and long drawn out, the sound of metal grinding on rock or coral, or metal bending and breaking, more and louder small explosions.

Adam landed on his hands and knees on a pile of gear and some marines and wasn't hurt.

Now the torpedo room started moving in a different direction. Slowly the front end came down. The marines who

were still on their feet walked down off the wall and out
onto the deck as, at last, the room stopped moving down.
For a moment longer it rolled a little from side to side as
though trying to find a comfortable place to rest, and then
all movement stopped.

For a little while longer the sounds outside went on but
then they, too, stopped and there was, at last, silence.

Adam pulled himself to his feet by the handle which
locked the door and looked around. "I think we're on the
bottom," he said. "Where's the chief?"

They didn't know. Slowly (and he wondered why he had
not noticed it before) he saw that Guns was covered with
blood, that Jason, hurt, was lying face down on the floor.
The Rebel, also hurt, had made it over to the lower rack
and was sitting down, his head in his hands, blood dripping
from his elbows.

A young corporal, his eyes wild, stumbled toward Adam
saying, "Let me out! Let me out of here!"

That started the rest of them. It was as though a quarter-
back had given the signal and the line was rushing forward.

The marines on their feet began yelling and pushing toward the door and, to Adam, they looked like wild animals,
their eyes crazy and wild sounds coming out of their throats.

Adam backed up against the door and held his hands out
as though to push them away. "Don't open this door!" he
yelled at them. "Keep the door shut!"

They hit him without seeming to know he was there,
knocked him down, pushed him aside. Then all of them began tugging at the heavy steel handle which turned and
.locked the door into its frame.

Adam crawled away from them, hoping that Guns or the
Rebel or somebody would stop them but Guns and the Rebel
and Jason were where they had been before. They were not

looking, they apparently didn't hear the yelling and cursing at the door.

"Chief!" Adam yelled. *"Chief!"*

No one answered and then he saw the rifle sticking up out of the tangle of gear. Adam pulled it free and got up on his feet. Holding the rifle low, he stood there and yelled, "Listen to me! Get away from that door or I'll shoot you! Come on, get away from it!"

It took them a few seconds for the words to get through to them and then they turned, one by one. They looked first at him and then at the rifle and it seemed to him that the wildness drained out of their faces and they looked like men again—scared men, but men.

"How do you know what's beyond that door?" Adam said, still yelling.

"My buddy's back there, flyboy," one of the marines said.

"The ocean's back there, too," Adam yelled. "Nobody's told us to open that door. This is their boat. Let them open it when it's time to open it."

A Pfc said, "I'm getting out of here, airedale," and turned back toward the door.

Adam rammed the rifle into his back. "There's nothing but water beyond that door. Go ahead, you stupid jerk, open it!"

The Pfc turned slowly around and looked at him. "Water?"

"That's right!" Adam yelled. He waved the rifle at him and said, "Come on, get away from it."

"Water?" the Pfc said, as though he could not believe it. Then, as he moved away, he looked down at the rifle. Very slowly he reached out and, delicately, with two fingers, pulled the oily rag out of the muzzle. Then, as though instructing Adam on the rifle range, he said, "Always remove any foreign material from the bore before you fire, Lieutenant."

"Thanks," Adam said, feeling foolish as he suddenly realized what he had done. He must have looked ridiculous standing there with a rag dripping out of the rifle while he threatened to kill these combat marines. Ridiculous. "Don't open the door," he said, mildly, and carefully put the rifle down on the gear at his feet.

5　As Jason wrapped a bandage around the chief's head, the marines who were not hurt stood silently around him, listening to him. Apparently the first violent explosion had knocked the chief down and, in falling he had hit his head on something, knocking him out. They had found him wedged under the torpedo-tube platform, bleeding from a cut in the back of his head.

"I think we hit a mine," the chief said. "I think that noise we heard—remember?—was a mine cable. You know what they do? They anchor these mines. They drop an anchor that goes down to the bottom but the mine doesn't come all the way to the top. The cable holds it down just far enough so you can't see it, but your ship can hit it. What I think happened is that we caught the anchor cable in the starboard bow plane—that was the noise we heard scraping on the boat, that cable. Then, when we rigged in the plane, it pulled the mine down on top of us. Back aft somewhere. It probably blew the whole aft end off the boat. Those mines can do a lot of damage." The chief thought about that for a minute and then said, "It doesn't take much of a hole in a submarine to get it into serious trouble."

"You think this is serious?" a marine asked.

"I think the boat's dead," the chief said.

"How about the people back there? My buddy was back there."

"There may be some people trapped in one of the other compartments like we are. Maybe in the after torpedo room. Maybe. But there's nobody alive amidships."

"How are we going to get out of here, chief?" Jason asked, tucking in the end of the bandage.

The chief looked up at him. "We aren't," he said.

The marines stood around in silence looking at the chief.

"Never?" the young Pfc said.

"That's right, sonny. Never."

The Pfc walked over to the other side of the room and sat down on the rack. "Gee," he said, "that's pretty bad."

"I wonder how deep it is?" Adam said, just for something else to say.

"What difference does it make? The only thing that makes any difference to us is, how long will the air in here last. That's the only thing. And it doesn't really make much difference. How deep we are doesn't make any difference at all."

Adam wasn't arguing with the chief, but it was easier to fix his mind on something which wasn't important than to let it go on and think about what was important. "It might," Adam said. "We might be only a few feet under the water."

"No," the chief said. "The last sounding I heard was a hundred fathoms, so we're at least that far down."

"How much is a fathom? Six feet?"

"That's right, six feet equals one fathom."

"Six hundred feet," Adam said, slowly realizing how far down that was. "That's a long way down."

"It doesn't make any difference," the chief said. "We could be a thousand feet, ten thousand feet down, it wouldn't make any difference."

A corporal said in a bitter, angry voice, "But this must have happened before. Don't they do anything? Do they just let people die?"

"It *has* happened before," the chief said. "Back at the submarine base in Pearl they have a big wall map of the Pacific and they have little submarines made out of magnets that they can move around on that map. Each little magnet has its name on it—and we're a little magnet with a name on it. And under some of the magnets they write, 'Overdue—Presumed Lost.'" The chief looked up at the marines and said, "I don't know why this is, but this seems sadder to me than other ships. When you're dead you're dead. But on surface ships when they go down somebody usually sees them and some of the people in them survive and they can tell the next of kin that the ship went down at such and such a place and what happened to it. In a submarine they just write that under the magnet. 'Overdue—Presumed Lost.'"

It was the word "lost," Adam thought, that was so sad.

It bothered the others, too. They stood around, looking at the steel walls, or wandered around, looking at the walls, or sat down and looked at the walls.

And then a Pfc said, "Hey, you guys. Look at this."

The Pfc was over by the door, staring at something, and some of the marines wandered over there. As Adam started to join them they began to back away as though a snake was on the floor, or something.

"What is it?" the Pfc asked, backing away.

"It's water," Adam said.

The marines stood far away and stared at the water. The chief got up off the bunk and came over and looked at it.

The steel door between the torpedo room and the after part of the submarine was a long oval in shape and it was set into the wall so that it was a foot or so above the level

of the floor. At intervals all the way around it were what
the Navy called "dogs." These were heavy steel latches working on an inclined plane so that, when the dogs where swung
over they put great pressure on the rim of the door, closing
it tightly in its frame of steel.

Now, in various places around the rim of the door, water
was coming into the torpedo room. It was coming in thin,
strong streams shooting straight out from the door, then
curving as it lost velocity and fell to the floor.

The streams of water were falling down on the combat
gear which, when the room tilted up, had all slid aft into
a tangled heap.

Adam moved a little closer and put the palm of his hand
out in front of one of the streams. It struck his hand with
great force, knocking it away. Adam, surprised by the force,
raised his hand and licked the wet palm. "Salt water," he
said to Jason.

They both turned then to look at the chief.

"I told you," the chief said, mechanically. "The boat's
dead." He turned and walked slowly back to the bunk and
sat down, all the marines watching him with interest.

Then Guns hollered, "Come on, you guys, we're not dead.
Stop up those holes. Come on."

Adam joined them as they gathered again at the door,
studying it.

Adam knew before they started that they were not going
to stop those streams of water. If they had been coming
straight through little holes in the door they might have been
able to stop them, but the water was coming from behind
the flange which overlapped the steel casing and there was
nothing they could do.

They tried. They kept working at it, jamming things into
the cracks, stuffing in rags, pieces of ramrods, pounding in

the lead of bullets. But no matter what they did the streams would break through, slamming against them.

At each failure they grew more wild until, at last, one of the marines grabbed a rifle from the mess and started hammering on the steel handles of the dogs with the butt, trying to force them to close more tightly. When the stock broke he kept on hammering, pieces of the rifle breaking off and flying around the room, the barrel bending, the forearm shattering.

"It won't work," Adam said, almost to himself and walked over to the torpedo tubes and sat down on the little raised platform.

As the marines moved around at the other end of the room, Adam could see the water either in streams or splashing down on the men and the gear.

He couldn't understand why, but somehow, the sight of the water made him feel—good. It was water, water from the sea. It was something he understood. Something he was familiar with. Unlike the whole nightmare—the combat gear, the combat talk, the rifles and the daggers—the water was real and not strange to him. It was the sea. The sea he had surfed on a thousand times, the sea he had been swimming in a million times, the sea he had watched for so many hours waiting for the surf to roll. Or just sitting on some beach watching the sea.

He knew full well that the water streaming past the door and now ankle-deep on the deck was a menace to his life. He knew that the water was going to keep on coming in there, rising to their knees, to their belts, to their chests and, finally, to their faces—their mouths and noses. He knew that the sea coming in here was going to kill them and yet, somehow, he felt good.

He raised his feet off the floor and sat on the platform, his arms around his knees, and looked at the water and wondered why it should make him feel good. Why, when he knew that the water was going to kill him, did he think that, somehow, this water was going to save his life?

The marines were still working at the door, slogging around in and on their soaking gear, tripping over their rifles, skidding on rolling helmets, falling and cursing and working.

And Adam sat there trying to think. And he couldn't think. All he could do was remember a crazy guy who used to bug the surfers (and everybody else) and, now, although he could see this guy clearly in his mind, he couldn't even remember his name.

A nut. A long skinny drink of water who always wore a beat-up old straw hat with a wide brim and all the straw coming out of it.

A nut. He had a theory a minute, this guy, and he would stand there in front of the surfers and yell at them.

Why those tigers didn't eat this guy alive Adam never did understand. The nut would stand there in that crazy hat and tell these surfers, these real tigers, that: (a) they were no-good bums or (b) hoodlums and (c) stupid, because they didn't understand these theories he had. But the surfers let him get away with it, Adam thought, because he was a goof, a nut.

What was that nut's name?

Adam looked down at the water, then looked intently at the steel walls. He didn't have time, he told himself, to waste thinking about a kook on a California beach a million years ago. This water was coming in here to kill them all.

Across from him Jason and the Rebel were talking earnestly to the chief.

The marine who had been hammering on the door dogs with his rifle now waded a few feet out into the middle of the room, and stood there looking at the remains of his rifle. "I've busted my rifle," he said, in a surprised voice.

Adam heard the chief saying, "Pump it out with what? Don't you know this boat is dead? They're dead back there. Everything's dead. The crew, the motors, the batteries, the pumps—everything!"

A marine said to his buddy, "I guess we're going to die in here." He said it exactly as he would have said, "I guess we're going on K.P. next week."

"Yeah, it looks like it," his buddy said.

The marine with the broken rifle walked over to Guns and said, "I've busted my rifle, Guns."

"You won't need it," Guns said gently.

"I sure busted it," the marine said and dropped it down into the water.

Rebel got up and wandered over to where Adam was sitting hunched up on the platform. Adam watched the water swirling around Rebel's legs, almost up to his knees now. Rebel leaned against a torpedo tube, looked up at the ceiling and said, "Ah nevah thought, when Ah was pickin' dat cotton and totin' dat bale, that mah life was goin' to be measured out in no feet and inches." Then he looked down at Adam. "She's going to fill right up, isn't she, Adam?"

"Not all the way," Adam said. "Most of the way, but not all the way."

"It don't make me no nevah-mind," the Rebel said and wandered away, saying, "Ah guess the South will have to rise again without me. I wonder what it looks like?"

"What looks like?" Adam asked.

"The South," the Rebel said, wandering back. Now the drawl was gone and he spoke in a flat, dry New England accent. "I've never been South. I've always wanted to go but the furthest south I ever got was Trenton, New Jersey. I'll bet it's nice down South. Magnolias and things."

Adam felt as though his mind belonged to someone else.

That it was out of his control. Things were drifting around in it that had no business there, no connection with this water, this room. He wished that he could make it work; make it *think*.

"You're pretty far south now," he said. "You're past the equator."

"I mean Dixie," the Rebel said, "'way down South in the land of cotton. I *been* past the equator."

That nut was telling the surfers that their surfboards were all wrong. Telling them that their boards should (a) be made out of fiberglass and (b) have just a little skeg [that's the way he talked—(a) this and (b) that]. He was a nut.

What was that theory he was yakking about all one summer?

Suddenly Adam remembered the nut's name. Thorenson. A skinny, intense kid who always danced around when he got mad (which was *all* the time). Adam could see him now dancing around in the beach sand wearing that straw hat and with his sleeves rolled down and long pants and socks and shoes, all full of sand, as he danced around and yelled at the surfers.

And now he remembered it all. The nut yelling it at them. Thorenson's Theory was: You are stupid to drown.

6   Adam climbed up to the top torpedo rack and perched up there, looking down at the water rising slowly in the room. Across from him the other marines had also gotten up on the top rack and looked, in the dim red light, like some sort of grotesque naked birds.

Jason was standing down in the water looking slowly around, his face a blank. He was holding his trouser legs out of the water with both hands like a kid starting to wade somewhere.

The chief was moving around in the water, sloshing through it as though, by ignoring it, he could make it go away. He was unwrapping the CO_2 absorbent cakes and spreading them around on the racks and tubes.

Thorenson's Theory.

Why was it, Adam angrily asked himself, that theories are always so easy to read and so hard to understand.

Okay, he thought angrily, so you're stupid to drown! But people drown. How did that nut think he could keep you from drowning?

Thorenson kept yelling at the surfers something about Somebody's Law. Whose Law? What did it say?

Jason, holding his pants up, waded over and climbed up beside Adam. He sat for a long time looking at the water and then said, "Isn't there something we can do, Adam?"

"There's a theory," Adam said, "but I can't remember it."

The chief finished breaking out the CO_2 cakes and started fishing around in his locker which was now more than half under water. Adam watched him idly as he found his .45 and then fished around some more until he found two clips with the slug-loaded bullets. The chief then climbed up with the other marines and started dismantling the gun.

Adam tried to remember the Law. Somehow he was convinced now that if he could work out Thorenson's Theory it would save his life. So—*think*.

The best he could do was to remember one day in a physics class in the Santa Monica High School, Santa Monica, California. Samohi, they called it. Just this one beautiful day and the '38 Ford pickup was parked down near Wilshire with his surfboard sticking out the end and Butch Lincoln (how did *that* cat manage not to go to school), was waiting for him and Adam was waiting for the bell and this teacher, Miss Marble, (No Marbles Marble), was going on and on about . . .

Was the guy's name Boyle?

Yeah, Boyle and another one, Charles.

He could hear Thorenson now, yelling at the surfers and dancing around. "(a) you're too stupid to know what Boyle's Law is and (b) you couldn't understand it if you knew it!"

What was Boyle's Law?

It had been a beautiful day and so, to pass the time, Adam started tossing his books out the window into a bed of geraniums. One by one, when No Marbles wasn't looking, he flicked the books out the window. But she *was* looking. . . .

One atmosphere equals . . .

"What's going to happen, Adam?" Jason asked.

"I'm just trying to think," Adam told him. "To remember. When I was in school."

"Think about what? I want to know what's going to happen *now!*" Jason complained.

"Well, it's physics," Adam told him. "That's what's going to happen. Physics."

"What's that got to do with *now?*"

"I don't know," Adam said, trying to remember what he had been thinking about. The Ford pickup and he'd heard some excited kid yelling outside the window, "Surf's up! Surf's up!" then this No Marbles tapped him on the shoulder . . .

The tech sergeant was standing down there in the water looking up at Adam. "What are we going to do, Lieutenant?"

"I don't know," Adam said.

"You *got* to know!" the sergeant yelled up at him. "You're an *officer!*"

"So, I'm an officer," Adam said. "That doesn't make me a genius automatically."

Jason leaned over toward the sergeant in the water and

said, "If he knew how to get out of here do you think he would be sitting here, stupid? Leave him alone. He's thinking."

Adam felt ashamed of himself and he didn't want Jason to find out that all he was thinking was about throwing some school books out a window on to some geraniums.

The sergeant waded back to the other side and climbed up on the rack.

The chief kept cleaning the gun.

The Rebel said, "I keep thinking about Willy on that sand bar at Guadalcanal. He knew we couldn't come get him, and he knew they were coming to kill him. And it was just a matter of time. That's all. A matter of time."

The marine who had wrecked the rifle began to jabber in a high-pitched voice. The Rebel leaned over to him and said, "Listen. You saw Willy lying on that sand bar. Did you hear a yip out of him all day long? No, you didn't. So don't let me hear a yip out of you."

"But I'm going to *die!*" the marine yelled.

"So what?" the Rebel asked, not disgusted. "Did you join the Marine Corps to live forever?"

Suddenly, and from nowhere, a formula jumped into Adam's mind. The pressure of water, he remembered, increases at the rate of .445 pounds per square inch per foot of depth.

He thought about that for a while, multiplying inches and square inches and fathoms. "You know something," he said to Jason. "We're under almost a million pounds of pressure."

Jason turned to stare at him. "What? How many?"

"Almost a million pounds. Each."

Jason didn't believe him. "How can that be? Nobody can stand a million pounds weighing down on him. A million pounds could crush steel, let alone skin and blood and a man's bones."

"I never was much good at arithmetic," Adam admitted. But the formula was there—he could see it as though it were written on No Marbles' blackboard—pressure per square inch of surface$=.445\times$depth in feet$\times$area in inches. A man would have about 2800 square inches of skin, Adam figured, so the pressure on him—and Jason—was now three quarters of a million pounds.

"If it was that much," Jason went on, "we'd all be flat. Like those guys in the cartoons who fall on the pavement and get up flat as a piece of paper."

"No," Adam said. "That's right and the reason we aren't flat is because we're made out of water and you can't compress water. What isn't water is full of air pressing out as hard as the air pressing in. So it doesn't make any difference how many million pounds as long as the pressure out is the same as the pressure in."

"Okay," Jason said, "we're not flat." He reached down to the water which was above the lower torpedo tubes now and gently moved it with his hand. "A million pounds," he said. Then he took his hand out and watched the little ripples die down until the surface of the water was as motionless as oily steel.

The marines were looking at it, too, as they sat crowded together in one big frightened mess on the torpedo racks.

"I don't mind dying *doing* something," Strings, the tech sergeant, said, his voice morose, "like getting killed in a fire fight. But this sitting here dying gets me down."

"How much longer you figure we got?" someone asked.

Adam looked at the still water, the lenses of the emergency lamps reflected perfectly in it.

The only movement Adam could see was a slow, creeping up the walls. He watched the level of the water reach the bottom of one of the dials near the torpedo tubes. Then it crept past the rim, crept over the face of the dial, crept on until the top rim of the dial made a little indentation in the water for a few seconds and then could hold out no longer. The indentation smoothed over, the dial gone below the surface.

"We got hit about half an hour ago," Adam said.

Guns looked down at the still water. "Then I figure another half-hour is all we got." He leaned out a little and spat down into the water. The spit created a few little circles of ripples and then they died and the water was flat and still again.

The water touched the bottom of the upper torpedo tubes, slid up over the bright steel, slid around the locking ring and kept rising.

"Nobody'll even know!" the rifle-swinging marine cried. "They won't even know where we went. Or what happened to us. My mother won't know."

"Somebody knows," Rebel said consolingly. "They know where they sent us. Only we didn't come back, is all."

"We never got there," Guns said. "We didn't accomplish a thing."

The tech sergeant said, "What are you griping about, Gunny? You're on borrowed time anyhow. You should've got it on Guadal a long time ago."

"The only thing I don't like is sitting here like a chicken on a roost," Guns said.

"You thought of anything, Adam?" Jason asked.

"Has the water stopped rising?" Adam asked.

They all looked at the absolutely still surface of the water, now covering all the torpedo tubes and lying just below them.

"Has the water stopped rising, chief?" Adam asked.

pounds could crush steel, let alone skin and blood and a man's bones."

"I never was much good at arithmetic," Adam admitted. But the formula was there—he could see it as though it were written on No Marbles' blackboard—pressure per square inch of surface=.445×depth in feet×area in inches. A man would have about 2800 square inches of skin, Adam figured, so the pressure on him—and Jason—was now three quarters of a million pounds.

"If it was that much," Jason went on, "we'd all be flat. Like those guys in the cartoons who fall on the pavement and get up flat as a piece of paper."

"No," Adam said. "That's right and the reason we aren't flat is because we're made out of water and you can't compress water. What isn't water is full of air pressing out as hard as the air pressing in. So it doesn't make any difference how many million pounds as long as the pressure out is the same as the pressure in."

"Okay," Jason said, "we're not flat." He reached down to the water which was above the lower torpedo tubes now and gently moved it with his hand. "A million pounds," he said. Then he took his hand out and watched the little ripples die down until the surface of the water was as motionless as oily steel.

The marines were looking at it, too, as they sat crowded together in one big frightened mess on the torpedo racks.

"I don't mind dying *doing* something," Strings, the tech sergeant, said, his voice morose, "like getting killed in a fire fight. But this sitting here dying gets me down."

"How much longer you figure we got?" someone asked.

Adam looked at the still water, the lenses of the emergency lamps reflected perfectly in it.

The only movement Adam could see was a slow, creeping up the walls. He watched the level of the water reach

the bottom of one of the dials near the torpedo tubes. Then it crept past the rim, crept over the face of the dial, crept on until the top rim of the dial made a little indentation in the water for a few seconds and then could hold out no longer. The indentation smoothed over, the dial gone below the surface.

"We got hit about half an hour ago," Adam said.

Guns looked down at the still water. "Then I figure another half-hour is all we got." He leaned out a little and spat down into the water. The spit created a few little circles of ripples and then they died and the water was flat and still again.

The water touched the bottom of the upper torpedo tubes, slid up over the bright steel, slid around the locking ring and kept rising.

"Nobody'll even know!" the rifle-swinging marine cried. "They won't even know where we went. Or what happened to us. My mother won't know."

"Somebody knows," Rebel said consolingly. "They know where they sent us. Only we didn't come back, is all."

"We never got there," Guns said. "We didn't accomplish a thing."

The tech sergeant said, "What are you griping about, Gunny? You're on borrowed time anyhow. You should've got it on Guadal a long time ago."

"The only thing I don't like is sitting here like a chicken on a roost," Guns said.

"You thought of anything, Adam?" Jason asked.

"Has the water stopped rising?" Adam asked.

They all looked at the absolutely still surface of the water, now covering all the torpedo tubes and lying just below them.

"Has the water stopped rising, chief?" Adam asked.

"Yes," the chief said, inspecting the barrel of the big, black gun then closing the slide.

Adam sat staring at the water and slowly realized why he couldn't understand something as simple as Thorenson's Theory. It was because he didn't want to. He didn't want to because, if he did, he might have to find out if Thorenson's Theory worked. That would take some courage. And what Adam now recognized was the fact that he didn't know whether he had that much courage. Simple as that.

Maybe the chief had been talking for a long time. Adam didn't know but he was talking now and Adam began to half listen to him.

The chief was saying, "I never thought this was ever going to happen to me. I don't know about you guys and what you talk about before you hit a beach or something like that, but in submarines . . . I guess I've heard it a hundred times. Always the same thing. You'd be sitting around somewhere and somebody would bring it up and you'd talk about it, each man giving his reason for what he'd do, but you never paid much attention. You were just shooting the breeze.

"But now it isn't shooting the breeze, so I'll line it out for you the way I've heard it a hundred times."

The chief pushed one of the ammo clips up into the butt of the gun and laid it down on his knees. "We're in the bind every man in the boats has wondered about . . . and wondered what he would do. We're down on the bottom, in deep water, with no chance of rescue, no chance of getting the boat up, with all the air you're ever going to get right here in this room. There's no food, which doesn't matter. But there's no water and no more air. What are you going to do?" The chief looked around at them and they, in turn, looked at him, or at the ugly black .45, or at the close steel walls, or at the still, still water.

"It's happened in other boats," the chief said. "I don't know what the guys did. Nobody will ever know. But when it's like this. When all you've got left is to go real fast or let it come real slow I don't think many guys waited for it. All I know is I don't want to take all that agony—for nothing. The foul air, the thirst burning you up. I don't want all that agony."

"Is that all we've got?" Guns asked.

"That's all," the chief said. He picked up the pistol and held it, lying flat in his palm. "We've got this . . . or sit here and die real slow, real hard."

"What about outside?" Adam asked.

The chief looked over at him, surprise all over his face. "Outside? Outside what, Lieutenant?"

"The sea," Adam said.

The chief put the gun carefully back down on his knees and then sat there, looking over at Adam. "I don't know what it feels like to have your lungs torn right out through your ribs, Lieutenant. And I don't want to know. You were right. There's a million pounds of pressure on us. You go outside and that pressure will tear you apart."

It was coming back. Bit by bit. Thorenson dancing around, kicking sand all over them and yelling, "Boyle's Law, you hoodlums!"

Adam looked across at the black gun and then at the walls, so close now all around him. They were not things that were familiar to him—a gun and a coffin.

He looked down at the water and thought that he had never seen water so absolutely still, so absolutely without friendliness. But it was water, it was the sea, and the sun could sparkle on it.

Adam was surprised to hear his own voice saying, "We didn't come here to shoot ourselves, chief."

The chief's voice was patient. "You're six hundred feet

down in the sea, Lieutenant. You leave this boat and you'll drown before you're halfway to the top."

"It's stupid to drown," Adam said, his mind back on Thorenson's Theory.

"It's stupid to be where we are, but we're here," the chief said. Then he shrugged. "Personally, I don't like the idea of dying that way."

"I'm not going to die," Adam said.

They sat over there, the marines and the chief, looking at Adam until finally the chief said, "I don't want to argue with you, Lieutenant, but there's a difference between what you're saying and what I'm saying. I'm saying you don't have a chance to live. You, nor any of us. You're telling these people that they can live—out in the sea. So they go out there and they die. What about that?"

Adam had not thought of it that way, but now he did. When he had thought it through he said, "No, I can't promise that you'll live. I can't guarantee that. But you'll have a chance to live. That's better than you've got in here."

"You don't have a chance, Lieutenant," the chief said. "Here's what's going to happen to you out in the water. In the first place, if nothing else was wrong, you'd just run out of oxygen before you could get to the top. You'd lose consciousness and drown. But there's a lot more going against you than that. If you leave the boat the pressure inside your lungs is going to be around two hundred and fifty pounds per square inch. As you go up that air is going to expand. I'll give you just one little example of how that air expands. With your lungs full of air—with as much air as they can hold without tearing apart—how far do you think you have to come up through the water for that air to rip your lungs out of your ribs? How far?"

The chief stopped and looked around at them but they did not answer.

"I'll tell you how far," the chief went on. "*Four feet.* Only four more feet! You may not know it, but if you could get a lungful of air at the bottom of an ordinary swimming pool, that air could kill you before you could get to the top of the pool. If expanding air can kill you in ten feet of water, what chance have you got in six hundred feet? Tell me that, Lieutenant."

Jason, beside Adam, said, "Is there a chance, Adam?"

"There's a chance."

Volume will vary inversely with the absolute pressure. Boyle's Law. The chief was right, the time of greatest danger would be at the end. When you could see the sun shining down bright through the water. When you could see the surface of the water itself like a mirror above you. That would be the time of danger. The air in your lungs would be expanding, doubling about every thirty feet . . . twenty times in six hundred feet . . .

And that would be the time when you were most afraid, most weary, closest to panic . . .

You could come up a hundred feet, two hundred feet . . . (Thorenson dancing and yelling that you could not exhaust all the air out of your lungs, that it was physically impossible to push it all out; there would be some left to keep you alive. If you didn't panic you could stay under for ten minutes. Fifteen minutes. You only drowned because you panicked) . . . five hundred and fifty feet, sixty, eighty, ninety . . .

And drown in the last ten feet.

Or—not drown. Live.

"Listen," Adam said, leaning toward the marines on the other rack, "all you've got to do is keep the pressure inside your lungs the same as the pressure outside, in the water. As we go up, let the air out. Keep letting it out all the way up."

"You'll run out of air. Then what?" the chief asked.

"No," Adam said, the vision of Thorenson strong in his mind. "You can't run out of air. There'll always be some left." (Thorenson had said if you had a cubic foot of air in your lungs at the surface and went down three hundred feet you'd only have a tenth as much air. That was important, but now Adam couldn't think why.) He said, "But we don't have to worry about that. It won't take long. It's only six hundred feet."

The chief was staring angrily at him. "I happen to know, Lieutenant, that the fastest a man can swim under water is about a hundred feet a minute. You think you can hold your breath for six minutes?"

"We wouldn't swim," Adam said, his voice vague. "Where are those life jackets?"

"Hey, look!" a marine said, staring at his wrist. "My watch is busted! But, look, it busted *in!* Everything's busted in, not out."

Adam looked at the man's watch, the crystal and face of it crushed in as though someone had stepped on it. And it scared him. The watch, sealed tight against water, had imploded from the difference in pressure. Just the tiny amount of air brought from the surface inside the watch.

That was what Thorenson meant. If you had a cubic foot of air in your lungs at the surface and went down three hundred feet you'd only have one tenth of a cubic foot. It worked the other way, too. If, under this pressure at six hundred feet you breathed in a lungful of air you would actually have twenty times as much air as you could breathe in at the surface.

Twenty times as much.

More than enough, Adam thought. The danger would really be too much, not too little, air.

"I think we can make it," Adam said.

One of the Pfc's said, "Who's this 'we' you're talking about, Lieutenant?"

Adam looked across at him and then at the others and then at Jason. They were now all strangers. Their faces were closed, their eyes were eyes he'd never seen before. They were strangers. "We've got to go," Adam said.

Guns leaned forward toward him and asked, "Are you saying that because you're an officer, Lieutenant?"

"Your officers are dead," Adam said.

The marines and the chief sat over there, watching him, studying him. And then the chief said, "Are you using your rank to tell these guys they've got some hope of getting out of this alive and then ordering them out to be killed in the water?"

"Chief," Adam said, "you and I are in the Navy. So—you keep out of this. This is for me and the Marines—"

Guns leaned forward again. "Are you taking command, Lieutenant?"

"You can call it what you want," Adam said. "But we've got to try. We've got to go, that's all."

The tech sergeant, Strings, now leaned forward. "Is that an order, Lieutenant?"

Adam had never given an order to anyone in his life, never taken command of anything and now he was confused. Until now he had never seen himself as an officer with the responsibility of his rank forcing him to order men to die.

Then Jason said, "That's an order!" He said it flat out and hard and then his voice changed and he said, "I don't know what's happened to you guys. Or what's happened to me. But I don't like it. He says we've got a chance out there. In here we haven't. What's the matter with you guys? *What's the matter?*"

The tech sergeant seemed not to have heard Jason. He

asked again, his voice a challenge, "Is that an order, Lieutenant?"

Adam looked back at him, trying, in his mind to straighten this all out. For them to stay in here was no good. And they knew it. It wasn't going to be good in the sea, either. Some —or all—of them might not make it.

He had the right, the authority, to order them out of the boat. The Marine Corps gave him that right, whether he wanted it or not. And the Marine Corps expected him to use it. But the reason, the purpose, the mission had changed. He was no longer ordering them to carry out a mission, whether they got killed doing it or not. He was dealing now only in the life or death of an individual, whose life or death would contribute nothing to winning or losing the war.

"No," Adam said and glanced apologetically at Jason. "It isn't an order. I'm going. You can go with me if you want to."

"It doesn't make any difference," the chief said. "It's all the same in the end."

"All right, you guys," Guns said, "the lieutenant is asking for volunteers."

"I'll go," Jason said.

The Rebel said, "It's against mah principles because the first law of the Marine Corps is to nevah volunteer for nothin', but Ah'll go wheah y'all go, y'all."

The tech sergeant surprised Adam by saying, "Why not?"

The master sergeant looked at the .45 the chief was holding and then at the water. "No," he said.

"No," one of the Pfc's said.

"No," the other one said.

"I can't swim," a corporal said.

"I can't swim very well either," the other one said. That left only Guns who was leaning back against the wall, looking up at the ceiling. They all waited for him and at last the Rebel said, "Okay, Guns, what do you say?"

Guns lowered his head slowly and looked around. " 'Say?' " he asked, surprised, "what is there to say? The lieutenant's a lieutenant, isn't he?"

7   The escape trunk of the submarine was a small steel cylinder set into the ceiling of the torpedo room and extending up through the deck. You got into this cylinder by climbing up through a round opening with a steel door in the floor of it. Another door, set low in the side of the cylinder, opened out to the sea.

Under ordinary conditions, with the submarine functioning properly, a man would go into the escape trunk, close the bottom door (which led into the submarine) and then, by turning on the high pressure air, he could equalize the pressure inside and outside the trunk. When these pressures were equal it was possible to open the side door and escape into the sea.

Now the chief turned from a bank of valves and looked at Adam. "You're lucky, Lieutenant. If you want to call it that. There's enough high-pressure air in the emergency bottle to get it on the bottom."

The chief made his way through the water to the handle which locked the bottom door of the escape trunk. He opened it, letting it swing down into the torpedo room.

Adam looked at the four marines—Guns, Rebel, Jason, the tech sergeant Strings—as they stood waiting. They had put on the yellow Mae Wests they were to have worn in the rubber boat to and from the atoll. They had not yet inflated these life preservers, but Adam had showed them the lanyards which, when pulled, would puncture the CO_2 bottles and inflate the rubber vests. All of them were wearing the two-piece green fatigues under the Mae Wests, but had on nothing else. No shoes, no helmets—none of the combat gear.

There had been a small argument about the rifles. Strings had insisted on taking his gun and ammo clips but Adam had finally persuaded him not to: they had a long way to go and they didn't want any more friction between them and the water than they had to have.

"All right," Adam said, "I guess we're ready to go. Just remember the one big thing. You're going out into the water with fifteen, maybe twenty times as much air as you're going to need. No matter what you *feel* like doing, no matter what you *think* you ought to do, don't stop blowing air *out*. Hold your head back, with your mouth open and keep that air coming out—*all the way up*."

He looked at them and saw their fear and felt his. ("Oh, Thorenson," Adam prayed, "please be right.") He tried now to sound like Thorenson; sound as though he really knew what he was talking about. "If you don't keep pushing air out *it—will—kill—you*. Okay?"

Strings pointed with his thumb up at the escape trunk, which was only a dark hole above their heads. "Once we're inside that thing we've got to go? Right?"

"Yes," Adam said. "So let's decide now how we go out— who goes first?"

"That's one good thing about the Marine Corps," the Rebel said. "Fall in line. You, being a lieutenant, go first, then Guns, then me, then Strings, then Jason."

"Then let's go," Adam said.

They did not move, but stood in the water not looking at him, nor at anyone else. They just stood there as though they were all alone in the whole world.

Then Guns spat into the water and reached up over his head and began climbing up into the escape trunk.

They went up one by one until only Adam was left. "Tell me again, chief. What do I do?"

The chief told him, slowly, counting off each procedure.

He was to close and dog the lower hatch. Next, he was to undog the lateral hatch and take it off the latch, but not open it. Then he was to admit water—slowly—through the sea valve. This, the chief thought, would take about a minute. When the water was above the top of the lateral door Adam was to pound on the walls as a signal for the chief to open the emergency high-pressure bottle.

"When the inside and outside pressure are the same the lateral door should open by itself: if it doesn't, *pull* it open."

"Thanks, chief."

Suddenly the chief stuck out his hand. "Good luck, Lieutenant," he said. Then he raised his head and looked at the faces of the four marines looking down into the submarine. "To all of you," the chief said. Then he added, "You're not going to make it, but it's as good a way to go as this. . . ." He patted the black gun in his belt.

Adam pulled himself up into the escape trunk, the marines helping him.

Down in the submarine the chief pushed the heavy, round steel door up toward the floor of the escape trunk.

Adam watched the oily steel rim of the door moving upward and as it moved it kept cutting off the view of the torpedo room, foot by foot.

It was, he thought, as though the world were being closed off from him, leaving him . . . where?

Adam, with hardly room to move, stooped and caught the moving door and pulled it all the way closed. Then he spun the dogging handle, feeling the dogs sliding out of the door and into the steel mortises in the deck.

The heavily lensed lights in the trunk had imploded, the lenses and bulbs bursting inward, but the battery-operated battle lanterns, which were not airtight and whose bulbs were spherical, still worked, throwing a dim and eerie blue light down on Adam and the marines crowded together in the steel cylinder.

Adam started to reach for the hatch latch but stopped. The marines had not said a word and were just standing there, the yellow of the Mae Wests looking bilious in the blue light. Adam straightened and looked at Jason. "What do the Marines say when they finally get into a fight?" he asked.

"You mean 'committed?'" Jason asked, his voice breaking a little.

"All right," Adam said, "when we let the water in we're committed. Until then we can . . . go back into the boat."

The marines didn't say anything, but they glanced at one another—quick, furtive glances, as though each one was afraid the other would see his fear.

"Then here it comes," Adam said, easing the dogs and taking the latch off.

As it had in the torpedo room, water began pouring in around the edges of the door. They stood watching it rapidly rising up the walls, rising up them.

"That stuff going to stop?" the tech asked.

"It should," Adam said.

"Theoretically," the Rebel said.

"I want it to stop right below my mustache," Jason said.

They looked at him and it made Guns laugh.

The water kept rising but finally stopped about eight inches above the top of the lateral door.

"We're about as ready as we're going to get," Adam said. "When you go, go fast. Duck down and move out of the door. Be careful not to snag the Mae West or let your clothes hang up on anything. When you're outside the boat I guess you'd better hang on to it until you get the lanyards pulled and the Mae West inflates. Then turn loose and *go*."

He stopped and thought a minute. There would be no

change of pressure until they moved upward. "While you're getting out the door and inflating the Mae West you won't have to let your breath out but, once you start up, start letting it out."

Jason's voice sounded far away and very small. "How long is it going to take, Adam?"

Adam remembered times in the water. Times when he had been wiped out on a surfboard and buried in the wave and his movement upward toward the surface had seemed infinitely slow. Then, other times, coming up from a free dive he had seemed to move very fast. But he did not know how fast they would move now. The expanding air in their lungs would make them buoyant and the Mae West would help.

"I don't know," Adam said. "It'll take a while."

"Like forever," the tech said.

"Maybe. I don't know. But we'll have enough air in our lungs to stay under for . . ." What had Thorenson claimed? And he remembered the kid yelling that, if he could get enough oxygen in his lungs, he could stay under water with only one breath for fifteen minutes. ". . . fifteen minutes," Adam said.

"I never heard of anything like that," Guns said.

"Let's go," Adam said. "Before you go under take a few breaths. Not too deep or they'll make you dizzy. Just slow, ordinary breaths. Then, don't rush anything—don't panic. Just move. But *move.*"

"I can't swim very well," the Rebel said.

"No swimming!" Adam said, again remembering Thorenson's Theory: this one about the viscosity of water. "Stay finned out. Except keep your hands straight up above your head. Keep your legs together and your feet pointed down. Try to shape up like a fish. We'll go up faster."

"You ever done anything like this, Lieutenant?" the tech asked.

"Not yet," Adam admitted.

"Well, I'm going to be in a hurry. So I'm going to help myself out a little. I'm going to swim."

"No," Adam said. "Don't do anything you have to think about because I think it's going to take about all you've got to keep the air coming out of your lungs. I think you'll go up faster not swimming."

"You go your way, I'll go mine," the tech said.

"Okay. You know exactly as much about all this as I do—as anybody does." Adam turned away toward the lateral hatch and began breathing slowly and regularly. He didn't want to hyperventilate. As nervous as he already was it might really spin him in, so he breathed only in shallow breaths.

In his mouth he could taste the stale, dead air which had already been used by four men and would be used again.

And it suddenly struck him that they would have to go up through the sea a distance longer than two football fields laid end to end; they would have to go almost an eighth of a mile . . . without taking a breath.

What if Thorenson was wrong and, somewhere along the way, they exhausted all the air in their lungs? What then? Adam knew, from feeling it many times, that the impulse to breathe *in* was almost insurmountable. Your entire body strained to take that breath. Only, they would be . . . where? With a hundred feet still to go? Fifty? It would be sad, he thought, if Thorenson turned out to be wrong during the last ten feet. That they would run out of air when they could see the sun shining down through the water.

And then Adam remembered a dog he'd had when he was a kid. A comical pooch who had picked up the name Barnstable.

And the high cliff in Pacific Palisades, a straight-up-and-down cliff which, if you were brave enough, you could go, on hands and knees, to the edge of and look down at the antlike cars moving on the Coast Highway far below. He remembered now, in this escape trunk with four marines, the shaking fear he had had as he edged his way out to the edge of that cliff.

But Barnstable was absolutely fearless and would go galloping past Adam to the very edge of the cliff and stand there wagging that nothing tail of his while he looked down in delight at the highway far below.

Adam turned and looked at Jason and was surprised to find Jason looking back at him. And Jason was scared. Adam could see that in his eyes. And Guns was scared. And the Rebel. And the tech.

"Listen," Adam said, "think the way a dog does. Don't think about what *might* happen. Just think about what *is* happening. That's the way dogs think."

Their eyes, looking at him, didn't change.

"Well, I guess I'll go," Adam said, turning away from them.

He lowered himself, bending his knees, and felt the water moving up his chest, up along his neck. To his chin, his mouth. He breathed once more lightly through his nose and went on down, the water closing over his head with a little swishing sound.

He was shocked to find that it was pitch-dark. He could not even see the outline of the opening in the side of the trunk but had to feel for it with his hands.

He moved out through the small opening and then caught the rim of the hatch to hold himself down. He did not yet begin exhaling, and would not until he started up and the pressure changed.

It was not quite so dark out in the sea. There was a dim, faint, sourceless green glow all around him. He seemed to be inside the light itself, not outside with it shining on him.

He could see very little of the submarine beyond the conning tower but it looked as though it had been broken apart
just behind the forward torpedo room.

Now the marines were coming out. In the dim light he
could not see their faces but recognized their shapes.

Guns came first and Adam could see one hand moving as
the other gripped the side of the door. Adam reached out to
him and found one of the lanyards and pulled it, hard. The
Mae West began to swell, a dull yellow blob and then Guns
suddenly streamed up past him and disappeared.

The tech came then, his Mae West inflating almost before
he got clear of the doorway. Then the Rebel. Finally Jason.

When Adam saw Jason's Mae West filling he pulled his
own lanyards, feeling the hard, upward tug as the CO_2 ex-
ploded into the rubber sacks.

Adam let go and was instantly surprised at the speed with
which he suddenly moved upward.

However, in a moment, the feeling of movement stopped.

Until now Adam had been afraid, but he had been too
busy to give it time. Now there was time and this sudden
sensation of being motionless in the water, *caught* in it,
brought a fear greater than anything he had ever known.
A fear which enveloped him with darkness—which seemed
to wipe out everything: thought, feeling, sight, everything.

Adam came out of it to find himself rigid in a strained
position, his hands and arms straight up above his head, the
palms together the way a girl holds them to dive. His head
was back, his eyes open, his lips open, but his teeth were
clenched together. His body, from shoulders to toes, was stiff
as a board.

Then he realized, with a relief which made him want to
yell, that *something* was moving. Air was gushing out from
between his teeth, billowing in moving grayish white clouds
over his face—he could feel the touch of the bubbles against

his skin. Then the air was streaming down past his neck.

For a second Adam lowered his head and looked down. The whole front of his body was covered with the foam of his exhaling.

He was moving! If he were not then the bubbles would be going up, not down.

And he was moving fast. From somewhere—not from No Marbles Marble; not even from Thorenson—an item dropped into his mind: bubbles come up about sixty feet a minute.

He was moving faster than the bubbles so he was going up faster than sixty feet a minute.

But how much faster?

By holding his head far back he could get his eyes above the cloud of bubbles foaming out of his mouth. Above him the world was a bright green glow with, suspended in it, four indistinct dark areas.

They seemed so far away from him; as though leaving him behind, alone. As though the marines were deserting him, leaving him down here to die.

Adam swung his arms down with one powerful stroke, his head still held back.

He ran into a trail of air bubbles which blurred his vision.

He stroked his arms again, turning out of the stream of bubbles, and came up alongside one of the marines.

It was Jason, who was not yet aware that Adam had pulled up alongside him.

It was not so lonely now with Jason there, the foam of bubbles from his mouth streaming around his chin and neck and down his chest. Not so lonely. As he looked up Adam saw that Guns and the Rebel were only a few feet above him, shrouded in the whitish-green stream of bubbles which looked almost as real as the crocheting his grandmother used to do.

And then Adam saw the tech. Far away, far above him.

The tech's body was a perfectly black shape and, as Adam focused through the salt water on his naked eyes, he saw that the tech was swimming—arms and legs moving rhythmically. No comet tail of bubbles was coming from him.

Adam watched him, wondering, and afraid again. Maybe the tech was right. Hold your breath and swim for it. The tech was certainly far ahead of them, far closer to the surface, to survival.

It bewildered Adam and confused him and he could feel his mind drifting off. *Feel* it, and yet he couldn't stop the drifting of it.

He was thinking about the bubbles which he could see streaming from Jason's mouth. Suppose, all of a sudden, no more bubbles came out of Jason's mouth, or out of *his* mouth. That when he tried to breathe out, to compress his lungs, none of the green-silver bubbles came out? Well, Adam thought, then that nut Thorenson was wrong. The pity of it is going to be, Adam thought, that I won't be able to walk out on State Beach at Santa Monica, California, and grab that nut by that crazy straw hat and tell him, "Back to the drawing board, you nut! Your theory doesn't work. I *drowned.*"

And then, as he looked upward, he saw the tech coming toward him. The tech was no longer swimming, no longer even moving. Bubbles were coming out of him but they were drifting upward. Not fast, just drifting, so that the tech looked as though he were lying in a cluster of soap bubbles, which Adam noticed now were not pale green like Jason's but faintly tinged with pink.

The position of the tech in the water was what brought Adam's mind roaring back from State Beach.

The tech was lying stretched out, on his back. He was not moving, not swimming.

Adam had seen two men die, both of them aviation cadets,

killed by their planes, and somehow because of the fire and the wreckage they had, for him, lost their identity as men. They had become part of the great wreckage of the planes.

But the tech was terribly dead. The explosion of his lungs had not disturbed the outer shell of his body. But he was dead, the blood-tinged bubbles still oozing out of his open mouth.

The tech went by him and Adam did not lower his head to look down into the blackness.

They went on, their trails of bubbles streaming down and dying. A feeling of weakness began in Adam now, a feeling which seemed to move through him with the flow of his blood. A threatening weakness because he could feel now that it took an effort to keep the air streaming out of his mouth. He could feel a dull, all-over ache in his chest and lungs and it didn't seem to him that as many bubbles were flowing out of his mouth as there had been before.

He looked over at Jason and the sight shocked him. Jason's head was down on his chest and his arms were half lowered and seemed to be adrift in the water.

Adam reached out and caught Jason by the short, stiff marine-corps-style hair and pulled his head back. Then he wrapped an arm around Jason's belly and pulled Jason hard against him, forcing the air out of his mouth in a burst of bubbles.

Green bubbles, not pink with blood.

Adam turned him loose and pushed him away.

And they went on up.

The bubbles from his mouth covered Adam's eyes now and he closed his burning eyes, feeling that he could not strain his head back far enough to get his eyes clear of the bubbles.

Anyway, he thought, what difference does it make?

Six hundred feet from the bottom of the deep sea was too far to go. So it made no difference.

After a long time Adam opened his eyes and, with great effort, forced his head back.

Something was wrong. Instead of the green world he had expected to see—green with the bubble-streaked bodies caught in it, there was a wildly shattered and broken silver mirror. A bright, silvery mirror with, right above him, some legs with bare, pale feet hanging down through the mirror.

Then Adam broke through the mirror and felt the soft, warm, fresh air against his face. He breathed it in slowly, riding high in the water with the Mae West shoving him up as though to get him completely out of the water.

BOOK THREE
The Deadly Shore

1   "Bretheren an' sisteren," the Rebel said, "that was the longest trip Ah evah took."

Adam and the marines lay exhausted in the sea, breathing the good clean air, floating in their yellow Mae Wests.

Jason said, surprised, "Hey, you guys. You know how long it took us to come up?"

"All my life," Guns said.

"No!" Jason said, holding up his arm with a watch on it. "It didn't even take *two* minutes."

"You're kidding," Adam said, amazed.

Jason looked at his watch, shook his arm, held it against his ear. "No, honest. I timed it when I left. It only took a minute and fifty-some-odd seconds. Not even two minutes." Then he said, as though not believing it, "And I feel fine."

Adam was floating near Jason and he felt fine too. "Thorenson," Adam said, "you *nut!*"

"What?" Jason asked.

"Nothing. Just a guy I knew."

Then Adam noticed the thin, pale trickle of blood coming out of Guns' ears and staining the water. "You okay, Guns?" Adam asked.

"My ears were giving me a fit, but they feel better now," Guns said. "How about you guys?"

Adam paddled himself around and raised himself up as high as he could in the water.

He knew that they were close to the island because of the wall of surf and spray and haze but, also because of those things, he could see no sign of land, nor trees, nor buildings —nothing. But they were close, floating just outside the breaking seas.

"The tech bought it," Jason said.

"He bought it. He swam and he didn't let the air out."

"That's a pity. He could have made it."

Guns looked all around and then down at his fatigues billowing around under the Mae West. "We made it," he said, as though just now realizing it. Then he raised his head. "I think we ought to get out of these Mae Wests, Lieutenant. You can see 'em for a million miles. No use coming all this way and get shot out here in the water."

"We haven't got far to go," Adam said. Then he held his Mae West up as far as he could and showed them how to deflate the things.

He felt much heavier in the water as the Mae West sank in a glowing yellow shimmer into the sea.

Now all of them were floating low in the water, only their heads above it.

"We should've backed Adam up," the Rebel said in his Yankee voice, and seriously. "We should've said, 'Yeh, that's an *order.*' Then maybe more of us could've made it."

"Maybe I should have made it an order," Adam said.

"No, Lieutenant," Guns said. "No officer I know in the Marine Corps would *order* his men to go on a thing like that when there wasn't any real use in it. You did right. But we should have made them come with us. Me and the Rebel and Jason."

"Maybe those guys will look at that old black .45 and get it on up here," the Rebel said.

"I don't think they will," Jason said. "There's nobody to show them how."

Guns turned over and looked at them. "They won't come," he said flatly. "I wouldn't either. Even knowing as I do now that I could make it, I wouldn't try it again, Adam. No, it was too hairy."

"I died eleven times," the Rebel said.

"I died *all* the time," Jason said. "It was hairy."

Guns suddenly began to laugh. "Man, this is the most formidable invasion force I ever saw. Four wet marines without a weapon in the crowd."

"So what do we do now, boss man?" the Rebel asked.

"We'd better stay out here until dark," Guns decided.

"No," Adam said. "With you bleeding, that isn't healthy. Anyway, we've got to see what we're doing when we go through the surf or we might not get through."

"Looks kinda rough," the Rebel said.

"Nothing looks rough to me any more," Jason said. "After that, nothing."

"Jason, boy," the Rebel told him, "that warn't nothin' but a little ol' swim."

"A million miles," Jason said. "Can they see us out here?"

"I don't think so," Adam decided. "Not unless they're really looking for us, expecting us."

"It's easy to tell," Guns said. "If things start going *chunk* and the water splashes around they've seen us."

"Let's go see what it looks like," Adam said. "I feel like stretching out on a beach somewhere and letting the flies walk around on me."

"No," the Rebel said, "Ah want one of those dusky maidens to fan off them flies."

Adam started swimming through the warm, clear blue water, and as he swam he noticed that the color was fading into a dark and then pale green and soon, down through it, he could see the roil of the surf's backwash.

He had not heard it before. Rather, he thought, he had heard it but had not registered it in his mind because he was then only happy to hear any sound at all. But now he heard and listened to it and paid attention to it.

The sound was in three parts—first, a low, steady, mushy roaring; then a slow beat of waves breaking; and then after each break the long hard rumbling of the water crossing the land.

The sound alone told him that it was a high, hard surf. The water was deep, right up to the coral of the island, so the waves swept in, long, unbroken and silent with no opposition from the bottom of the sea until they met the sudden, shallow barrier of the coral.

Here, where they swam, there was almost no indication of wave action. Their bodies rose slowly and fell slowly in a smooth surging motion and the water, in the windless air, was as smooth and pretty as tinted glass. They rose, they fell, and the surf ahead of them seemed disconnected from the sea they were in.

As Adam approached the line of the surf he began to realize that getting through it was going to be almost, if not more, dangerous than the ascent from the submarine. The waves were booming like cannon and he knew that these shore-breakers were high and fast, breaking straight down on, he suspected, the coral barrier reef, not on sand.

But, Adam remembered, if the operation plan called for going into the lagoon at sunset they must now be twenty or thirty miles from the lagoon entrance where the surf would be milder or, perhaps, nonexistent. Twenty or thirty miles was too far, too risky and, anyway, there would probably be people on the beaches there. Here, he hoped, with this surf constantly breaking there would be no reason for people to be wandering around.

"Is that thunder?" Jason asked.

"Waves," Adam said.

"What are we going to do?"

"A little plain and fancy surfing, m'boy," Adam said. "Yes, a little surfing."

He swam on toward the island, watching the surf ahead and now feeling the smooth pull of the water trying to draw him on toward the rising wave, or draw him back as it fell.

He let himself be carried up almost to the break of the crest and, from there, he looked down.

He had never in his life seen a wave break more vicious than this. From the crest he stared almost straight down for, he guessed, forty feet. Stared down at bare, broken and dead coral with only trickles of the previous wave running in it. As he backed off, the wave broke, curling almost straight over and falling. It hit the land with a force so great that Adam could feel the shudder of the land in the water around him.

These waves were impossible. As he swam away from them he felt a bitter, mean defeat attacking him. There should be a reward now, he thought bitterly: we've come out of the submarine. We came six hundred feet from the bottom of the sea and we lived. Can't we rest now? Can't we lie on the beach he had seen beyond the coral and rest? Be rewarded for what we've already done? Why must this line of surf hold us out here in the sea after what we've done?

As he swam away from the roar of the surf he knew that those waves were impossible, their threat to his life greater even than the six hundred feet.

"How does it look?" Jason asked.

"A little rough," Adam said.

He swam on past the three marines, swimming away from the island until, when he looked back, he could not even see them except when their heads came up on the high swells of the sea.

Now he looked back at the white curtain drawn between him and the land, looking for some break in it or, if not that, then at least some small place where it was not so high, so furious.

He remembered now seeing on the aerial photographs of this island the extending white areas on the seaward side, little finger reefs of coral sticking out from the shore a little farther than the rest of the formation. Perhaps, with these finger reefs breaking the wave action, the surf would be less monstrous between them.

It was hard to tell in the high haze of water and the white blasting of water beyond the blue backs of the waves but, as he watched, he thought he saw two places where the waves broke a little sooner.

Adam swam back to the others. "All ashore as is going ashore," he said.

"Ah'm ready," the Rebel decided. "In fact, Ah *been* ready."

"Any of you been in heavy surf?" Adam asked.

"Ah was knocked down by a wave," the Rebel told him. "Ah was three years old and that was a *mother* of a wave!"

Adam looked at the other two and they shook their heads. "There's a way to get through it," he told them. "I remember my flight instructor telling me that when you get in trouble in a plane the best thing to do is turn loose the stick, shut your eyes, relax and hope for the best."

They followed him along the roaring line of the surf until he could see one of the finger reefs sticking out almost in front of him. He led them around that and on until they were about halfway between the two reefs. Then Adam turned and started swimming slowly toward the shore. He took them in as close as he could, but still free of the wave pull. "Anybody want to go first?" he asked.

"I don't know, Lieutenant," Guns said. "Do you think it would look good for the Marine Corps for us non-commissioned officers to invade this island and then you come along behind? You think that would look good?"

"It would look better if I didn't get there at all," Adam told him. "Only I haven't got any place else to go."

"Ah'm all for education," the Rebel declared. "Mah pappy used to say, 'Son, if'n you don't learn something today, Ah'm goin' to knock you down to stump size.' That's what he said."

"I don't mind going first," Jason said. "Somebody's got to." He was looking at the wall of the surf, his eyes very serious about it.

"Have you gone through surf like this?" Adam asked.

"I got ashore at Guadalcanal."

"Son," the Rebel said, "you was in a *boat* at Guadalcanal. I bet the highest surf you ever saw was when your maw threw you in the bathtub."

"Okay, Tarzan, you go," Jason said. "You so big and brave."

"We're wasting time," Guns said. "What's the trick, Adam?"

"It's a one-time thing all the way," Adam said. "Once you're in it, there's no way back out. I think the marine word is 'committed.' So don't try to fight your way out of it even if you think you've goofed and can get out. You can't. The next thing is to go with it; just stay loose and go with it. Most of all, don't look at it. I mean, when you go in, don't look down. You won't like what you see and you might try to back out of it."

A wave struck the beach with a roar so loud that it drowned out what he said next and, more than that, scared him. Even between the finger reefs these waves were monsters, rising high, breaking, falling straight down on bare coral.

When the noise subsided, Adam started again. "Waves come in sets," he told them. "Six, seven, a dozen at a time, then there's a little lull. In each set there's usually one that's a good deal bigger than the rest and the one after that one is the smallest. That's the one we're looking for. I've been watching, and these waves seem to be coming in, nine at a time and the seventh is the big one. It's not a law, but that's what it looks like. So watch 'em, so, when you hit, maybe there'll be some water left from the big one."

"Why don't we all go, together?" Jason asked. "You can tell us which one to take and all."

"No," Adam said. "One at a time, so if one of us gets through he can help the others."

"What do you mean 'if?'" the Rebel asked. "Is it that tough?"

"It's tough," Adam said. "Now, when you pick the wave you want—take it. Start going with it, but stay back a little from the front—you don't want to be the first thing to hit the ground.

"When it starts to break, the top, where you are, will begin to roll over. As soon as you feel it really rolling, get all the air you can and then pull yourself up into a ball. Make a tight ball and stay tight—*all* the way. If you come out of that ball with your arms and legs sprawling around it's going to break you all to pieces. No matter what happens—and it's going to be a long ride—stay in the ball.

"Next, after the wave strikes you'll be deep in the soup. This stuff can kill you even quicker than water because you think you can breathe it but if you do the drops of water in it take you right out. So get all the way out of the soup before you try to breathe."

"They gonna serve us soup when we get ashore?" the Rebel asked.

"Yeh," Adam said. "Soup made out of a couple tons of wave churned into nice salty foam. You'll like it, Rebel. Only —it'll kill you if you stay in it."

Adam looked at them, three serious faces just above the level of the water. "Here comes a set," he said, beginning to paddle toward shore. "Remember, don't look down, stay balled up and get out of the soup."

"Bye, bye, Lieutenant," the Rebel said.

2 When you looked toward the shore the oncoming waves didn't seem to exist; it was just rolling blue water suddenly exploding. Now, though, Adam was close to the break and was treading water, waiting, and looking back toward the sea.

From here it was different. He could see the monsters as their backs began to hump up, blue and slick. They seemed to rise out of the calm, unmoving sea as though some enormous animal was inside them, struggling to get out of them. And the sea could not contain them for, behind him, Adam could hear the roaring of the animals as they broke loose.

He waited, watching, and the three marines farther out lay in the water watching him.

The set was coming in steadily, a long reach between each wave, and he counted them as they moved smoothly under him, each one tugging at him as though trying to lure him to destruction.

And then the seventh one began to rise, humping up huge and blue from the flat sea, going higher and higher. As it swept past the marines it lifted them up into the sky and, to Adam, it looked like a moving wall of water.

He backed away from shore, afraid of the big one's pull,

but it passed under him and crashed with a shocking sound behind him.

The next one was here, smaller, lower.

Adam turned and swam with it, swimming hard for he wanted his speed to reach that of the wave's so that he and the wave would move together and thus the wave would throw him farther out of the sea.

As he swam he could feel the wave bunching up under him, coming up and up like a bucking horse, the muscles of it growing taut as though the water was changing into a fluid steel.

The thing was going up into the sky at a fearful rate, higher and higher and now it had gripped him and he knew that there was no use swimming any more.

And he was beyond the point of return. He was, as the Marine Corps put it, committed to this wave. He would either live or die with this one, no other.

The crest had not yet started to curl over and he was in thin water, a long, thin, greenish ridge of water which seemed to be trying to break loose from the great body of the wave below but could not.

Adam hoped that the others would not do as he was doing now, for his eyes were open and he was looking toward the island.

He was looking *down* on a thick grove of coconut palms, their long drooping fronds motionless in the windless air.

Water from the seventh wave was still high up on a sandy beach but, as he looked down at it, he could see that it was already draining back through the coral of the reef which lay between the sea and the sand.

This was not the first wave Adam had ever ridden in to the shore. He had surfed hundreds, thousands of them from the sea to the kind California beach with its long sloping bottom. He had surfed big ones, the man-killers, and he had been afraid in the moment of taking them, and afraid during the wild, wild voyage with his body half out in front of the wave and the thing roaring and clawing at him from behind.

But this thing he was in now was horrifying. As he looked down, the front of the wave was a smooth blue straight-up-and-down wall of water reaching from the high sky to the naked coral far down there below him.

Don't let them look, he prayed. Make them keep their eyes shut. Or they'll fight the wave and get caught in the front of it and it will slam them down and kill them.

All along the top of the high blue wall now a feather of white water was beginning to form, racing along. The wall itself was curving smoothly seaward, the solid bottom of it like a gigantic foot being pulled by some force away from the shore.

Adam pulled backward with all he had as the feather of white swept across his back. He could hear the hiss of the crest beginning now to break as the curving wave rolled downward upon itself.

He rode it, feeling the tremendous strength of the thing around his body. He rode it, watching and listening to it, and feeling it—feeling its growing speed, growing strength; feeling now his body moving not only forward but down.

He remembered a wave once which had thrown him completely out of itself. Thrown him straight up out of the water as though it personally found him distasteful.

He remembered that and got deep into this wave so that it could not throw him away.

It was almost silent, only the hissing of the crest and a wet, slithery sound, and the drier sound of the coral, beaten dead by previous waves, rattling wetly far below him as the wave swept forward over it.

And now he was truly going down, the feel of it a movement faster than a plane, even an SBD, in a steep dive or even an uncontrolled fall. He and the wave were falling and falling, the hard, rocky coral rushing up at him, the trees, a greenish-brown blur rushing up past him.

Adam waited, listening and sensing the movement and gauging until he felt that it was time to tuck.

From then on, until it killed him or threw him up on the shore alive, there would be nothing more he could do. Nothing.

Adam drew his legs up now and wrapped his arms tightly around them, jamming his knees against his stomach. Then he lowered his head and rammed it in against his kneecaps and felt the water fold around him.

It was dark blue in here and noisy and fast moving.

The wave had him now completely and was rolling him over and over.

Then the blue was gone, the noise was wet and huge, there was violence all around him and the wave slammed him down on the coral.

He landed on his back and shoulders with such force that it almost tore loose the grip of his hands locking his knees against his belly. He heard the air rushing out of his lungs and clamped his mouth shut.

Then he was rolling through a turmoil of soup and sand and huge pieces of coral, rolling over and over.

Then it was quiet, with only the sound of water trickling somewhere.

Adam loosened his hands slowly, then slowly straightened his legs. No really great pain stabbed him. He hurt; his back hurt and his head hurt and his knees and elbows hurt and he could see that they were bloody through the torn green cloth. He sat up and looked toward the sea and saw the next wave curling right on top of him. He spun around and, on his hands and knees, crawled away from it and on up into the surprisingly hot, dry sand.

There was nothing in that wave. Nor the next. Adam got up and walked through the receding water and looked at the next monster curling down, looking through the great blue body of it.

Someone was in it; he could see the darker, blotchy outline of one of them.

It was Jason who hit so hard that it broke his grip, flattened him out and shoved him, rolling over and over, appearing and disappearing in the soup.

Adam got him by the belt and hauled him clear and flung him up on the sand.

Then Guns came, neatly rolled, and made it.

And the Rebel made it.

Bleeding, cut, scraped, bruised and battered, the four men dragged themselves across the sandy beach and into the shelter of the palms.

The enemy could have taken them then with ease for, suddenly, as though it had been waiting, a total exhaustion swept over them all and they collapsed, lying sprawled and bleeding among the palm trees.

3 The three enemy soldiers stood looking down at the sleeping men sprawled in the dusty sand with flies walking around on their wounds. To the enemy the four men looked harmless; they had no weapons of any sort; they had been injured, for each was stained with blood; they looked helpless in their torn clothing, their bare feet lying on the sand.

But the enemy soldiers had seen the USMC stenciled on the torn clothing so they stood back from the sleeping men, each of them holding his rifle on them, cocked and ready. In low tones they discussed the sleepers and decided not to kill them now but to take them to the island's headquarters.

These harmless, helpless, hurt men could be of value to the Emperor; they would have information about the war plans of the United States. And there were methods for making these men reveal all the information they had. Methods.

In the early morning there was still some mist of the night left drifting around the trunks of the palms and the heat of the day had not yet begun.

The only English word these soldiers knew was "Okay." One of them said it loudly now. "Okay! Okay!"

Guns, the Rebel, Jason and Adam woke up. They turned over in the sand and looked up the barrels of the small-caliber rifles, the wood of the stock almost yellow.

The leader of the enemy patrol made a get-up motion with his rifle and said, "Okay."

The night before, sitting under the palms and drinking coconut juice from the fruit, there had been not an argument but at any rate a heated discussion about what they should do.

Guns had said, "The first thing we've got to get is weapons. Something to shoot. If we can't get that, then a knife. But *something!*"

They had not moved far from where they had come ashore. Just back into the concealment of the jungle beneath the palms.

"We'd better get sort of organized," Adam had said.

"That's what I mean," Guns told him. "First, get something to shoot. Then scout this place and find somewhere to hide."

"As long as they don't know we're here, we don't need weapons, Guns," the Rebel said, forgetting his southern drawl. "We need food and water and a place to stay."

"And some shoes," Jason put in.

"Shoes."

"We're not going to be here *forever*," Guns said. "Shoes

can wait. What we want is something to protect ourselves with."

The whole thing seemed to Adam a little pointless. Maybe they were just arguing because they felt as he did. Cheated. Tricked. After what they had already accomplished—the ascent from the boat, the survival through that surf—they felt that they had done enough. Instead, they were hopelessly trapped on this enemy-held island.

"What chance of them coming to get us out of here?" the Rebel had asked.

"The submarine was supposed to do that," Guns said. "But they must have another one standing by. They must have."

"I don't think so," Adam said. "If they knew four of us were still alive they might send a sub for us, but they don't know that. In a couple of days they'll put one of those 'Overdue—Presumed Lost' tags beside our names and that'll be that."

"Do you think that?" Jason asked.

"He knows that, Jason," the Rebel said. "We're going to be on this stinking island until the war's over. And that's going to be a *long* time."

"So maybe we better get organized," Adam said. He looked over at Guns in the moonlight. "We don't need weapons right now. We need a place to hide and something to eat and water. Those first."

"Okay, so we're wandering around here barefoot as a yard dog and they jump us. What do we do without a weapon?"

"The main thing is, don't let them jump us," Adam thought. "We're a lot better off if they never find out we're here."

"You know it," the Rebel said. "We haven't got a Chinaman's chance if they even *think* we're here. This island isn't big enough to hide us if they ever start looking for us."

"Yeah," Jason agreed, "they mustn't know."

And now they *did* know. Adam sat up in the sand, his whole body stiff from the slugging the sea had given him, and looked at the little round ring of the rifle muzzle, and looked up into the face of the enemy.

For a moment it was easier just to accept this thing. Adam knew what the end of it would be, but he felt in this moment that he had fought all he could fight—from the sunken boat to here. He had gone as far as he could. He had nothing left. It was not fair, he told himself. It wasn't fair at all.

Beside him Jason, the Rebel and Guns sat up and stared at the enemy, each one with the gun slanting down.

Adam studied the faces of the enemy. He had seen faces like this many times before. The faces of the workers, the men of the rice paddies and farms, the mills and mines. Not the faces of the university students, the city dwellers.

Adam straightened his back, sitting up firm and upright. Then he scowled at the enemy and said, in their language, barking it at them, "Attention! Stand at attention, you low peasants!"

They moved slowly, dumbly. But they moved. They lowered the rifles, put their feet together, straightened up, all the while staring at him.

"We are officers in the Imperial Navy," Adam barked at them in their language. "Now! About . . . *face!*"

They turned their bodies slowly around but their heads lingered, their eyes still looking at him. Adam saw the doubt beginning to form and he knew that, in a second, these men would come out of the spell authority in a loud voice had put on them. In a second they would wheel back around with the rifles.

But Guns said, in a whisper, the words very urgent, "Get 'em!" and Jason, Guns, the Rebel moved.

For a moment the low mist was disturbed by the violence

and swirled around. Deep furrows appeared in the loose dry sand where feet strained against it. There was almost no sound. Heavy breathing, a dry gargling, the wet breaking of small bones.

Guns stood with one of the rifles in his hand examining it and said in disgust, "Filthy."

Adam had never seen a thing like that and for a moment it sickened him, but then he thought of the bright rings of the gun muzzles. This is the way it has to be, he thought. This way. You, or him. There was no other way.

He knew, too, that if he was going to survive in this place he must, soon, learn how to use such violence with such control. Jason, the Rebel and Guns had done it so fast and with no confusion.

"Let's get these people out of the way," Guns said. "When they don't report in there's going to be trouble."

"They're going to suspect. They're bound to," Jason said. "Look, some of that submarine is going to wash ashore, isn't it, Adam? Enough anyway to make them suspect something. Especially if a three-man patrol just disappears."

"You should've thought of that before we jumped 'em," Guns said. "Then we wouldn't have jumped 'em and they'd have killed us. Okay?"

Adam thought of the sea, of some faked accident. Jason was right, there would be debris from the boat—it was probably on the beach now. Perhaps there had even been some sort of signal from the mine.

They could not handle an alerted enemy. Three marines and a naval aviator with three rifles not much more powerful than a .22 couldn't handle an enemy suspicious and searching for them.

He went over to the first man on the ground and rolled him over. There was no sign of his death on him.

In one of the pockets Adam found what he had expected

to find and he held it up for them to see. "See if the rest of 'em have one of these," he said.

Guns, the Rebel and Jason leaned down to look at the little ivory rod Adam held. It was about the size of a thick cigaret, made of plain ivory. On one end of it was an intricately carved seal.

"This is the way they sign things, letters and things," Adam said. "With sealing wax. Maybe they've got that, too."

There was sealing wax on one of them, and a pad of the thin brownish rice paper. And the pen.

Adam sat down on the sand with the pen and paper and the three seals and the wax and began to write slowly in Japanese. He wrote the same thing on three sheets of the paper, writing: "I am a coward, unworthy of serving the Emperor." Then, using a different seal on each sheet, heating the wax with a flimsy little box of matches, he stamped each one.

"Now let's take 'em over under the trees," he said.

"They committed suicide," Guns said.

"That's right," Adam told him.

"They're great for that," the Rebel said, pulling a long, slim knife out of a sleazy wicker scabbard. "We found lots of 'em on Guadalcanal."

"They slit their stomachs," Jason said, his face grey and his eyes averted.

"Yes," Adam said. "Let's give them as much dignity as we can."

4   The marines and Adam had been on the island for six days now and each, in his own way, was losing hope of ever leaving it alive.

They lived in the jungle like slowly starving animals; forced to live this way by the enemy who completely surrounded them, forbidding them food from the sea, forbidding them fire to cook with or warm themselves by after a night of cold rain, forbidding them any avenue of escape. Their wounds from the coral cutting them when they came ashore were infected now, painful and bloody; they had been stung and bitten by every bug and insect infesting the dank jungle; fungus diseases were appearing on them—spreading areas of rottenness which seemed intent on eating them alive.

On the first day a new patrol had found the dead men with their letters to the Emperor and would have accepted their deaths as suicide except, by then, there were oil stains on the beach from the ruined submarine, there were bits of cork and other debris. Not enough, the men hiding in the jungle were glad to see, to tell the whole story, but enough to start a search through the jungle.

For two days the marines and Adam had eluded the search parties who came streaming through the jungle, passing through it from one side to the other. They had eaten little in those days and slept little, and when the search was finally abandoned they collapsed in the ruins of a native house and slept for a day and a night, taking turns on sentry duty all the time.

There were things other than coconuts and bitter-tasting roots to eat but they were not yet starved enough to tackle the big, greasy lizards they sometimes saw. The Rebel had almost managed to eat one that he caught but the sight of its tail slithering away all by itself was too much. Or, perhaps, just the sight of the dead lizard's raw, still quivering body was uninviting.

They could have eaten the huge land crabs they sometimes saw scuttling around at night. But they, too, were uninviting and with a rank, penetrating odor. Without fire to warm the things the men could not, yet, eat them.

The only birds were birds of the sea which did not fly into the jungle, nor lay their eggs there.

After six days the marines and Adam were discouraged. This island was a mess.

They were huddling now in what shelter they could find from the cold night rain. They had eaten the coconuts they lived on and were trying to sleep—to reach another day— and Adam wondered what for?

Around the burned-out native house they had set up dried palm fronds in a circle, balancing them so that if anyone coming toward the house stumbled into the fronds they would rattle and fall. Inside this circle one of the marines or Adam walked sentry duty, two hours apiece, all night long.

One of the marines—or Adam. Adam still felt the hot flush of embarrassment when he thought about that. It had been either the first day or the second when Guns had said something—they would have to shape up, or something like that. And he had added, "You, too, Lieutenant."

Adam had told him, "Knock off the 'lieutenant' stuff, Guns. I just appointed myself a buck private in the Marine Corps."

They had been walking stealthily through the jungle but now Guns stopped and turned slowly around and looked at him.

It was then Adam realized that he'd said the wrong thing. The marines had all stopped and looked at him.

Finally the Rebel had said, "You've got a ways to go, Adam, but you're doin' real good."

Guns hadn't said anything.

Jason had tried to take the curse off it. "As far as I'm concerned," Jason had said, "the Marine Corps is someplace else. Me, I'm on this stinking island and so is Adam. He can be commandant of the Marine Corps if he wants to."

The nights were a misery, the rain turning everything to

mud but not stopping the crawling of all sorts of unseen and wet, slimy things which bit and stung. Sleep was hard to come by, for they were hungry with, now, a constant, unsatisfied hunger which no amount of coconut meat seemed to stop. They were cold, and wet, and sick—their sores and infections seeming more dreadful in the dark than even in the day when they could see the spreading diseases.

The nights were bad and the days little better. Each day working parties of the enemy entered the jungle to collect the fallen coconuts. (The marines and Adam, hiding from them, watched resentfully as these men gathered up their food and carried it away.) There was no freedom of movement, no time when they could relax this around-the-clock vigilance.

They were trapped in a small area of jungle which the enemy had left standing on the center of the island. The island itself was a long, thin strip of land lying between the open ocean and the atoll's lagoon. It must have once been completely covered with the coconut palms except for a small area on the lagoon side where the natives had lived. It must, Adam thought, have been a quiet and peaceful place—a little South Seas paradise. It wasn't any more.

Straight through the coconut grove and from one end of the island to the other, the enemy had bulldozed the trees away and then laid down an airstrip made of layers of crushed coral they had dug up from the reefs and the floor of the lagoon. On the seaward side they had left a remnant of the trees (and this is where Adam and the marines now sat in the night rain) which completely concealed the airstrip from the view of submarines or even surface ships.

The airstrip lay between the sea and the lagoon, a long, white scar, two hundred yards wide and, Adam guessed, at least five thousand yards long—long enough and solid enough to handle multi-engine planes.

Adam remembered now the almost fearful awe he had felt when they had first seen the long runway. And seen what was on the other side of it.

The enemy had here, on this island, an installation comparable to Ford Island, in Hawaii, or even some of the air bases in the States. There were hangars, camouflaged and buttressed with logs and sand. There were shops and warehouses, permanent buildings, some of concrete. The barracks and mess halls were well made, of wood—there were no tents, nor lean-tos; everything was solid and permanent.

Guns had been awed, too. The lagoon side of the island bristled with guns, all of them on concrete pads and well protected. There were dual-purpose AA guns, their long, canvas-hooded muzzles pointing toward the sky. There were many large-caliber coast-defense cannon—Guns guessed that some of them were sixteen-inchers, as big as the armament of battleships. In pillboxes all over the place were light and heavy machine guns, mortars, and light field artillery.

There were well-made, all-weather supply roads to the guns and pillboxes and, they suspected, underground tunnels as well.

The equipment they had on this island was formidable too. Bulldozers, earth movers, cherry pickers, a gantry crane, trucks and vehicles of all sorts.

Dominating the whole island was a square, solid, windowless concrete building, two stories high, squatting beside the runway at about the middle of it. On top of this was a glass-enclosed control tower with the radar antenna rotating above. The only openings in the massive concrete walls were narrow slits for the gun barrels.

"A battalion of marines with everything in the book couldn't knock out that thing," Guns decided as they had hidden in the jungle looking at it.

"Bretheren and sisteren," the Rebel had said.

They had spent an hour there, watching the enemy across the shimmering runway. There was activity everywhere—men, armed and in complete uniform, parading around in the sun. Men working in the repair shops. Trucks and cars moving about. The whole scene seemed to Adam to have an almost feverish, excited quality. It wasn't the way they did it in the Navy. These people were moving too fast, they were too busy.

And there were hundreds, thousands of them. Everywhere you looked there was the enemy.

Everywhere. As Adam and the marines had moved through the long days, they had found the enemy. He patrolled every inch of the perimeter of that island, from the seaward coral reefs around to the sloping smooth sand of the lagoon side. (Adam had said, "It's a wonder we got ashore at all with sentries all over the place.") His guns were manned, his lookout stations occupied. Patrols on foot and in cars moved all day long (and the marines were now convinced, all night, too).

At one time there had been a population of natives. On the lagoon side they could see the charred stakes of the burned-out grass houses and, in the jungle, there was the remains of the house they used for sleeping. A very long house of some sort had once been here, but it was now burned down. Around it were the burned remains of dugout canoes. Digging around in the remains had brought the marines and Adam nothing. An elaborately carved wooden chest, charred but not burned, had contained nothing useful.

The chest was, apparently, the property of the medicine men, as it held cloaks made of bird feathers and strands from the palms, with terrifying wooden masks painted in vivid colors. Jason had tried on one of the masks and found that the thing fitted on his shoulders with peepholes for his eyes at the bottom of it, the face of the mask being two or three feet above him. Jason danced around awkwardly in the thing, saying, "Abacadaba. I'm putting a hoodoo on the enemy. Their feet are going to fall off right up to the ears."

There were no natives on the island now and Adam wondered if they had been killed or transferred to some other island either in this atoll, or some other enemy-held place.

This was the largest island in the atoll and Adam and the marines had been dismayed by what they could see of the other islands ringing the enormous lagoon. Sand spits. Small, yellowish low mounds in the blue water of the lagoon. Barren, waterless, uninhabited and uninhabitable.

The two-hundred-yard-wide runway lay between them and the lagoon (and to where could they escape even if they could reach the lagoon's calm water? To the waterless and foodless sand spits?)

One day Adam had wondered about escape by plane and they had made their way to the downwind end of the runway where they had seen high revetments half concealed in the jungle.

The planes—there were nine of them—were the single seater enemy fighters; "Zeroes" was the navy code name for them. Even if he could take off in one of them, and it would have to be alone, Adam had thought, what good would it do? The fighters had a range of about three hundred miles and there was no land, of friend or foe, within three hundred miles of this island.

"Ah hates to say it," the Rebel now said, spitting out some rain, "but Ah thinks we all's in a little trouble. Ah *do*."

Jason said, "Rebel, I know people who'd give a million dollars for a tropical paradise like this."

"Then let 'em take my place," Guns said sourly. "Okay, you guys, I'm sacking out. Reb, you take the first watch, Jason the second, I'll take the mid-watch and you take the dog, Adam."

This was another long, cold, wet, miserable night. Those asleep did not sleep well for they were hungry, and more racked out from the ordeal than they thought, and more fearful than they would admit, even to themselves. And those who stood watch in the rainy darkness, standing against a palm tree trying to hear anything moving through the rain, could not help thinking, in the darkness, that here on this island, trapped, they were going to end their lives. Perhaps tomorrow, perhaps in a week but, certainly, it would not be long. The worst part of those thoughts was that they, who had courage, who had strength, who had training could not, in any way, prevent the taking of their lives. Neither by force (against so many?) nor by guile (outwit hunger and thirst?) could they prevent it.

There was no escape from this island.

5   In the radio room at the submarine base at Pearl Harbor a chief radioman relieved the heel-and-toe watch on the frequency assigned the boat on the Operation Moondance job. "Anything?" he asked.

"Nothing," the first class radioman said, taking the padded earphones off one at a time, slipping them over the chief's ears so that there was no span of time when someone was not listening on the Moondance frequency. The chief got into the high swivel chair, made a tiny adjustment of a dial, listened, looked at the jerking second hand of the clock above him. It was ten minutes after eight in the morning. . . .

In the Personnel Office a lieutenant (j.g.) who wore glasses came in and hung his overseas cap beside the white hats on the rack and sat down at his desk. In a moment a a first class yeoman came in and said good morning. The lieutenant (j.g.) said, "Anything?"

"No, sir."

The lieutenant (j.g.) took off his glasses and wiped them carefully with a white handkerchief and then put them on again. "Then you'd better pull the jackets of the crew, Bill."

"I have, sir."

"The officers?"

"Them, too, sir."

"What do you think? Should we go ahead with the telegrams, Bill?"

"Get 'em typed up anyway, sir," the yeoman advised.

"All right. MIA for all of them."

In the yeoman's office a third class was already typing up the form telegrams: "The Navy Department with great regret informs you that your —— (son, father, husband, brother) is missing in action. . . ."

Another third class came in, sailed his white hat at the rack, missed, picked it up, hung it up, looked at the third class typing and said, "You homesick or hungover?"

"I'm typing MIAs," the third class said.

"Oh," the other one said. . . .

In the Marine Corps Personnel Office a staff sergeant was eating out all hands. Usually he was a good joe but this morning he was prickly. "The Moondance detachment had twenty-three people. What have you chowder heads done with one of them?"

"Honest, Sarge," the bravest corporal said, "the roster is two officers, twenty men."

The sergeant leaned over the corporal's shoulder and looked at the list. "Oh, *no!*" he said. "Gunny Gibbs. With that nose." He read on down the list, slowly. "Ezra Stiles? Stiles?"

"The Rebel," the corporal said.

"Oh, *no!*" the staff said and read on. And stopped. "That kid, Jason. That kid saved my life on the Ridge."

"MIAs, Sarge?" the corporal asked.

In a fury the staff sergeant yelled. "Who said they were dead? So MIAs, chowder head. And you'd better find that other guy or I'll have your stripe!"

In the C.O.'s office at Adam's squadron the C.O. was on the phone with the officer in charge of the BOQ. "Adam Land? I don't know where he is, nor when he's coming back."

"What'll I do with his gear?"

"Pack it," the C.O. said.

"Ship it home?"

"I don't know. No, store it. I just don't know where he is."

"A guy can't just disappear."

"Adam Land did," the C.O. said. . . .

In the office of the Commander, Submarines, Pacific, an admiral stood at a wall mural of the whole Pacific Ocean area. Now he reached up and put a little toy submarine with a magnet in it on the mural. He put it beside an island marked MOONDANCE. Then, below the submarine, he put a little sign: OVERDUE, PRESUMED LOST.

The marine corps colonel watched him do this. "They were the best men in my outfit, Admiral."

"It's been eight days," the admiral said. "There's nothing else we can do."

"Another submarine?"

The admiral shook his head. "If any of your people, or ours, got ashore, the enemy will be alerted now. A second boat wouldn't have a chance. If they didn't get ashore . . . then the boat's gone, with all hands. We can only wait, Colonel."

"Have you any idea what may have happened, Admiral?"

The admiral sat down and looked out the window. "We never do," he said. "The boats go out there. Some come back. The ones that don't . . . Well, they just don't come back."

6 The long night somehow ended. As the sun began to sift through the darkness Adam went over to Jason who was sleeping, sitting half slumped at the base of a tree, the rifle across his lap. Adam shook him by the shoulders.

Jason came awake with the rifle in Adam's stomach. Then, as he slowly lowered the rifle, he drew in a long, slow breath and let it out as slowly. "Stand behind a marine when you wake him up, Adam," Jason said.

Adam could still feel the sharp muzzle of the rifle in his gut. "Yeah," he said.

They woke up the Rebel and Guns.

The rain had stopped, but it was not important. The four men stood, with nothing at all to do, in the low, thick mist the sunlight was pulling up from the rotted vegetation on the ground. The mist came only up to their shoulders.

Guns looked slowly around at the jungle, the brightening sky through the high fronds. Then he said quietly, "I sort of wish I'd stayed with the others. In the boat."

Jason looked at him and said, "Yeah?"

"Yeh," Guns said. "The war must be over for them by now. All over. And they're better off than we are."

"You think so?" Jason asked.

Guns swung his hand slowly around. "This place isn't big enough for us and them, too. No matter what we do, we can't take 'em all. There'll be some left to get us. Just like the air in the boat—it's just . . . how long? That's all, how long?" Then he turned and looked at Jason. "I tell you one thing, Jason. They're not going to take me alive. And if you've got any sense you won't let 'em take you alive either."

"They're not taking me alive . . . or dead," Jason said.

The Rebel walked a little way in the mist and then came

back. He stopped in front of Guns and looked at him for a moment. "Ah'm breathin', Guns," he said quietly. "In the boat, they're not breathin'. So now, we've talked aplenty." He swung around to Adam. "Any ideas, Adam?"

"Fresh out," Adam said.

"Maybe we could build a boat," Jason said. "I read somewhere that that's the way these natives got here in the first place. They drifted here in boats."

"The trouble is," Adam said, "the way we'd drift would be just deeper and deeper into trouble. They are on every island from here to China."

"We build a boat and then what?" Guns asked. "Do we carry it right through their lines and put it in the water and say tally ho. I tell you there's nothing we can do. *Nothing!*"

"We can keep breathin'," the Rebel said. "An' Ah'm tired of ham and eggs for breakfast. Think Ah'll have me a nice coconut for a change." He disappeared under the layer of mist, searching the ground for a coconut.

The mist burned off, the day went on. Now the strip of palms between the sea and the airstrip had become more familiar to them—it was their home. They were shadows among its shadows, movements with the wind movements of the leaves above them. Here, in this pale, hot, green place they were fairly safe.

To Adam it was exactly the same safety a man has who is standing in front of a firing squad. You are safe . . . until the triggers are pulled.

They were wandering in their green home, miserable and sick, hungry and defeated, alert for the sound of the enemy but, gradually, almost wanting to be found—to end all this.

And then they heard the music.

6 The long night somehow ended. As the sun began to sift through the darkness Adam went over to Jason who was sleeping, sitting half slumped at the base of a tree, the rifle across his lap. Adam shook him by the shoulders.

Jason came awake with the rifle in Adam's stomach. Then, as he slowly lowered the rifle, he drew in a long, slow breath and let it out as slowly. "Stand behind a marine when you wake him up, Adam," Jason said.

Adam could still feel the sharp muzzle of the rifle in his gut. "Yeah," he said.

They woke up the Rebel and Guns.

The rain had stopped, but it was not important. The four men stood, with nothing at all to do, in the low, thick mist the sunlight was pulling up from the rotted vegetation on the ground. The mist came only up to their shoulders.

Guns looked slowly around at the jungle, the brightening sky through the high fronds. Then he said quietly, "I sort of wish I'd stayed with the others. In the boat."

Jason looked at him and said, "Yeah?"

"Yeh," Guns said. "The war must be over for them by now. All over. And they're better off than we are."

"You think so?" Jason asked.

Guns swung his hand slowly around. "This place isn't big enough for us and them, too. No matter what we do, we can't take 'em all. There'll be some left to get us. Just like the air in the boat—it's just . . . how long? That's all, how long?" Then he turned and looked at Jason. "I tell you one thing, Jason. They're not going to take me alive. And if you've got any sense you won't let 'em take you alive either."

"They're not taking me alive . . . or dead," Jason said.

The Rebel walked a little way in the mist and then came

back. He stopped in front of Guns and looked at him for a moment. "Ah'm breathin', Guns," he said quietly. "In the boat, they're not breathin'. So now, we've talked aplenty." He swung around to Adam. "Any ideas, Adam?"

"Fresh out," Adam said.

"Maybe we could build a boat," Jason said. "I read somewhere that that's the way these natives got here in the first place. They drifted here in boats."

"The trouble is," Adam said, "the way we'd drift would be just deeper and deeper into trouble. They are on every island from here to China."

"We build a boat and then what?" Guns asked. "Do we carry it right through their lines and put it in the water and say tally ho. I tell you there's nothing we can do. *Nothing!*"

"We can keep breathin'," the Rebel said. "An' Ah'm tired of ham and eggs for breakfast. Think Ah'll have me a nice coconut for a change." He disappeared under the layer of mist, searching the ground for a coconut.

The mist burned off, the day went on. Now the strip of palms between the sea and the airstrip had become more familiar to them—it was their home. They were shadows among its shadows, movements with the wind movements of the leaves above them. Here, in this pale, hot, green place they were fairly safe.

To Adam it was exactly the same safety a man has who is standing in front of a firing squad. You are safe . . . until the triggers are pulled.

They were wandering in their green home, miserable and sick, hungry and defeated, alert for the sound of the enemy but, gradually, almost wanting to be found—to end all this.

And then they heard the music.

7 Along the edge of the runway tall, coarse grass grew four feet high. Adam and the marines lay in this stuff now watching the goings-on across the strip.

A band, the musicians in white uniforms with bright-colored sashes, stood near the concrete control tower, their brass instruments glinting in the sunlight as they played. The music floated across to the men lying in the grass but did not cheer them.

From the barracks area now columns of men, marching, appeared and formed in ranks behind the band. The men were in field uniform, armed and carrying packs and wearing steel helmets. The officers, however, were in white uniforms with sashes and sword belts, complete with swords. Adam could hear them barking orders at the men.

"Maybe they're getting ready to leave. For good," Jason hoped.

"It's a parade," the Rebel decided. "In the middle of a war—a parade."

"What war?" Guns asked.

The men across the runway relaxed now, but stayed in ranks.

"They're waiting for something," Adam said.

"For that old 'hup two three four,'" Jason said. "One thing, I'm glad to find out that the Marines Corps isn't the only outfit that marches around in the heat of the day, going nowhere, doing nothing."

"Sloppy outfit," Guns growled, looking at the thousands of men in ranks. "I'd like to get hold of that bunch for about five minutes. I'd shape 'em up."

"Listen!" Jason said.

There was the sound of heavy motors starting up, then idling back until there was a steady, level roar of them.

"Sounds like it's coming from that clump of trees," Jason said. "To the left of that gas dump."

Out from under the trees a tank appeared.

Jason whispered, "Look . . . at . . . that."

From the clump of trees the tank emerged, a steel elephant rumbling out of the woods, the long-barreled turreted canon swinging stiffly from side to side, the clank of the tracks and roar of the motor coming loud across the runway. It was unbuttoned, the crew standing in the hatch.

"Take a look at those ribbons," Jason said in disgust.

The tank crew was wearing what looked like football helmets. And from the top of these helmets there were gaily colored, thin streamers of cloth streaming out in the breeze.

"Now ain't that a real pretty sight," the Rebel said, as disgusted as Jason.

"Oh, Mama, buy me one of those," Guns said, turning away from the sight.

Behind the tank, field artillery appeared, then armored cars and troop carriers. They formed a long line in front of the troops, then, one by one, the motors stopped.

The marines and Adam lay in the grass, their uniforms torn by the coral of the beach and damp from the rain and sea, their faces stubbly with unshaved beards, their only weapons the knives and small-caliber guns of the enemy. They were hungry and weary, barefooted, bareheaded, infested and sick; lying in the grass looking across at their enemy.

"If we could get that tank," Guns said, lying in the grass looking at it.

"Now that's the way to go home," the Rebel said. "Drive home in a nice tank. How far you think it is to Pearl, Adam?"

"Too far for a bridge."

Guns looked at them angrily. "When are you guys going

to get it through your thick heads that we aren't going anywhere? Ever! But, get that tank. Open up with everything it's got. We wouldn't last long, but we'd take some of them with us."

Jason sounded surprised. "You mean, just get in and start shooting?"

"That's what I mean. Before they got the big guns turned around on us we could do some damage. Some real damage."

Jason looked at Guns. "What for?"

Guns stared at him. "What *for*? What are you in the Marine Corps for?"

"I don't know," Jason said. "To win the war, I guess. But what good would it do to get in a tank and kill some of them before they kill us?"

Guns turned over in the grass and said patiently, "You miss the point, Jason. They're killing us now. Just as much as if they were standing here starting a trigger squeeze. Who wants to go slow this way, like rats or something? We're going anyway, so let's go fast and loud, and take some of 'em with us."

"Sssh," Adam said, raising his head to listen.

Now there was a new sound. Adam twisted around in the grass so he could look up into the sky. "Betty," he said.

"Your lil' ol' mind is wanderin', son," the Rebel said. "You gotta watch that."

"Mitsubishi," Adam said, looking up.

"What would you say the caliber is on that tank, Jason?" Rebel asked.

"Big enough," Jason said.

"A ninety-six dash four. I *think*," Adam said.

"Big as one-fifty-five?" Rebel asked.

"Naw," Jason said.

"With two Kinsei Mark Fours," Adam said.

"Those machine guns don't look so heavy, either," Jason decided. "Around twenty-millimeter."

"They got a high rate, though," Rebel said, remembering the scream of those machine guns on Guadalcanal.

"Yeah, they can pour it out," Jason agreed.

"Fourteen-cylinder, air-cooled radials. A thousand horses apiece at ten thousand feet," Adam said.

"You're wanderin', boy," the Rebel said.

"Seven-hundred-and-eighty-gallon tanks," Adam said.

"*What* kind?" Jason asked.

"At two hundred miles an hour that's five hours," Adam said.

"What are you talking about, Adam?" the Rebel asked, serious now.

Adam sat up in the grass so he could watch the landing. He sent messages to the pilot—don't miss it, buddy. Come in smooth and easy and way down. Take it all, buddy. Use it all. Nice and easy now. Don't prang that lovely airplane.

The pilot may have gotten the messages, for he brought the big twin-engined plane down on the runway with only a little squeal of the tires, two little spurts of rubber burning before the wheels could start to roll. Nice landing.

"You've got to hand it to them," Adam said. "They make beautiful airplanes."

The marines watched the plane rolling down the runway, then watched it slow and turn and taxi back toward the control tower.

The band was playing. The troops were stiff and straight in ranks. The officers stood, waiting the command to draw swords.

Adam looked at the lovely airplane, listened to it; wondered what it felt like to fly. Then watched as the engines stopped and the life seemed to drop out of it.

Seven hundred and eighty gallons.

"Admiral, or something," Jason said.

Adam studied the Betty, now parked, engines stopped, in front of the control tower. The side door opened and a small group of men in blazing white uniforms began climbing out of it down a stepladder arrangement from which gaily colored streamers blew in the wind.

A truck appeared now, coming out of the tank park. It was loaded with fifty-gallon drums and as the white-uniformed men moved over toward the troops, now at rigid attention, the truck drove up near the plane and men with long hoses climbed up on the wings of it.

At first the idea Adam had seemed wonderful, but it didn't last long. All he had to do was look first at the thousands of armed troops over on the other side of the runway and then look at Guns, the Rebel and Jason—and at himself. Four ragged, beat-up guys squatting in some tall grass. Once they showed their faces every gun on this island would train on them, every man's hand would be against them.

The idea was nonsense. And yet it persisted. The plane was there, beautiful in the sunlight, with the men in the truck hand pumping gasoline into the wing tanks. Seven hundred and eighty gallons of it; a thousand miles through the sky; a thousand miles from this place.

"It's not going to be here long," Adam said.

"Probably the high brass out here to throw a brace into this outfit. He'll shake 'em up good and then fly away," Guns declared.

The band was playing again and the flags were flying.

Nonsense. Suicide. Even if he could get into the plane, Adam decided, it wouldn't do much good. He probably couldn't get the engines started before they would riddle the plane with gunfire.

Even if he could get it off the ground without being fatally hit what good would it do? The nine fighters in the revetments would swarm all over him before he could go twenty miles.

There was no use dreaming.

But the plane was *there*.

"If we could get our hands on that plane. . . ." Adam said.

They turned to look at him and the Rebel said, "Can you fly that thing, Adam?"

"It's got wings," Adam said.

"No. Honest. Can you fly it?"

"If I could get in it, I could fly it."

"Then let's go get it. You all," the Rebel said.

"I'd forgotten you were an airedale," Guns said. "You can really fly it?"

Adam nodded, watching them pumping gas into the plane. "The only thing is, we wouldn't get far with the fighters on our tail." He turned and looked at them. "Without them, and in the air, we'd have a chance."

"How much chance?" Guns asked.

Adam shrugged.

"Who cares?" Jason asked. "On the ground we haven't got any chance at all. So let's see what we can do."

"The fighters first," Adam said.

The marines and Adam had almost reached the first revetment when Jason, who was leading, slid like molasses down to the ground and disappeared into it. Silently and not moving fast Guns and the Rebel dropped out of sight.

Adam, seeing nothing, slid behind a tree trunk and waited.

But there at the end of the revetment, in plain sight, was the enemy lighting a cigaret. He was wearing one of the long-billed green caps, a rifle was slung over his bare shoulder and his rather baggy pants were stuffed into the tops of heavy gray socks. He had on tennis shoes.

He lit the cigaret, took a puff and then, hitching the rifle into a more comfortable position, made a sloppy about-face and walked slowly out of sight behind the revetments.

Guns, Jason and the Rebel sifted back to Adam. "Now we know there's one. Maybe more," Jason said.

"Let's go get him," Guns said.

"Maybe Adam ought to get him," the Rebel said.

Adam looked at him, wondering.

"Maybe there's two or three of 'em, Adam. We ought to find out. You could go talk to him in his lingo and be looking around before you take him. Then we'll know what to do."

Adam looked down at his uniform, the USMC stenciled black and clear on the jacket. He started unbuttoning the jacket. "I'll get shot in this," he said.

"Yeah," Guns said, "you might."

Adam stripped off the jacket and trousers and stood there in the faded green drawers, barefooted, bareheaded, wounded.

"That'll surprise him," Jason said, looking at Adam critically.

"Here," Guns said, pulling out of his pocket a still damp red bandanna. He knotted the corners and put it on Adam's head.

"Not so regulation," the Rebel decided, tilting the bandanna over Adam's eye. "You look great."

"It even surprises me," Jason said. "You look kind of silly. And that's good. You sure don't look dangerous."

"Here's a knife," Guns said. "Hold it up along your arm."

Jason must have read Adam's face. "You ever use a knife, Adam?" he asked. When Adam didn't answer Jason gently took the knife out of his hand. "You don't hold it that way," he said. "You hold it with the blade pointing away from your *thumb*, not your little finger. You don't stab, you shove it, Adam." He put the knife back in Adam's hand.

"It's hard to get it through the ribs," Guns told him, "so go up under 'em."

"It's hard to kill a man with a knife," Jason said, "but it'll make him bend over. Then clock him behind the ear. With the side of your hand. Not your fist."

"All right," Adam said, knowing that he was in a dream.

"Make sure there's nobody else around," the Rebel said. "We don't want no musket firin'."

"But take him out," Guns said. "Don't fool around with it."

"All right," Adam said. He bent his wrist up until he felt the point of the knife against his skin below the elbow. Then he moved out toward the end of the revetment.

Guns, the Rebel and Jason watched him go. "I hope he does all right," Jason said.

"He better," Guns said.

"He's never been in a fight in his life," Jason said. "No kind of fight at all. Maybe we better help him."

"We don't speak that lingo, Jason. How can we help him? We'd only mess up the whole thing."

"I guess you're right," Jason said, watching Adam walking toward the revetment, the red bandanna on his head looking ridiculous.

8   It was the longest walk Adam had ever taken. Somehow all the surface nerves of his body seemed now to be separate from him and from each other. Every nerve was feeling, all by itself, the sudden impact and pain and horror of a bullet striking it.

It was hard to think as he walked through sunlight and shadow; walking slowly and (he hoped) nonchalantly. He didn't want to startle the man. To surprise him, yes. But not frighten him. He didn't want to appear suddenly in front of the man. Nor did he want the man to see him from a long way off and have that much time to study him before he spoke.

From some memory, from some time in his youth in Tokyo a song—complete with words and music—came into his mind. A song about the samurai with their two broad swords moving through the cherry orchard always protecting the precious lives of the daimios.

Adam began to sing the song. Not loud. He stood at the end of the revetment, hidden by it still, and sang the song about the brave samurai and all their swords. He sang it slowly, listening between the words, until he heard the footsteps coming.

It was good. The footsteps were purposeful but not hurried.

It was like the last second when a monster of a wave is right there and you decide to take it. A little second of absolute weakness and then, when you've committed yourself to the wave, a good feeling.

Adam sauntered out from behind the revetment, the bandanna at a jaunty angle.

It was nicely timed. The sentry was three paces away from him, the gun still slung over his shoulder.

From here Adam could look down the line of revetments, see the engine nacelles of the planes, the chocks at the wheels. He saw no other sentry, nor any sign of mechanics.

"Oh, ho, you fortunate person. Good morning," Adam said to the sentry, using the dialect of the servant class. He could feel the knife sharp against the skin of his underarm.

The sentry bowed slightly, puzzled, but polite. "Good morning." He didn't come any closer and now his hand moved up to the stock of the rifle. Not fast, but moving there. "Fortunate?" the sentry asked, not understanding.

"That we are not standing stiff as ramrods with our knees

shaking like leaves in a high wind," Adam said. As the man looked down the runway toward the white uniformed ranks Adam looked along the revetments again. No one moved in the hot sunshine.

Adam took a step closer. He knew he was close enough now. He could see where the man's rib cage stopped and the soft, faintly hollow belly began. The long knife could go in there and go up under the ribs. It could go a long way.

"Who are you?" the sentry asked.

The man, uncertain, was easing the rifle sling off his shoulder. Now he put both hands on it. A marine in that position could swing that rifle down and kill you in a fraction of a second.

But Adam stood there, grinning, the knife now swung around behind his back. "I'm going for a swim in the Emperor's ocean," he said.

"Who are you?" the sentry asked.

Now the rifle was moving and he had to do something.

Adam stepped forward, spun the man around and then tried to clamp his arms to his sides. The small man was much stronger than he had thought, and very quick. For a second he was free, his arms free, as he turned back toward Adam, the gun sling slipping down his arm.

It did not feel at all as Adam had thought it would feel. There was no great, terrifying pain; even the impact was not great. He felt a burning sensation and a hard tap against his skin and that was all. The sound of it was flat, small and dull against the steady roar of the sea, the sound of the wind in the palms.

He discovered that he had dropped the knife.

The man was out of his hands now, out of reach, and Adam wondered why he felt a little dizzy.

The man raised the rifle and pointed it straight into Adam's eyes and then, slowly, as though making a ceremonial bow, the man leaned forward. He kept on leaning, falling to the ground, and Adam could now see Jason moving toward him, stepping over the dead man on the ground. Jason took Adam by the arm, his hand strong on Adam's arm. "Any more?" Jason whispered.

"No. I don't think so."

Jason pulled him into the revetment and hustled him along to the rear end of it. "You better sit down," he said.

Adam felt grateful to him for that and grateful that Jason helped him down to the ground or he might have fallen. He seemed now to have no strength at all.

The Rebel and Guns came sliding around the open end of the revetment. With their rifles low and ready, they backed toward Adam. Jason said, "He doesn't think there're any more."

Guns asked the Rebel, "Any sign they heard the shot?"

"Doesn't look like it. The band's playing."

"Keep watching," Guns said and then turned to Adam. He looked down at him, squinted his eyes shut, shook his head hard for a second and opened his eyes. "See if there's any first aid in the plane," he told Jason as he kneeled down beside Adam.

"Lean over, Adam," Guns said, and helped him lean far forward. "Good thing that wasn't a Garand," he said, pushing Adam upright again. "Cough as deep as you can and spit."

The cough sent a huge, tearing pain all through Adam and as he spat on the ground he looked down at himself.

It wasn't even dramatic. Nothing spectacular. Just a small round purple bruise on his skin with, in the center of it, a blackish dent, now oozing blood. "Went right through you," Guns said. "Didn't even make much of a hole coming out. You're not spitting any blood. How do you feel?"

"Not bad."

"Can you get up?"

Adam pushed himself upward. Guns helped him. For a moment he was dizzy and the pain in his side was great.

"Feel like anything tearing loose?"

"No." Adam took a few steps. "It just hurts."

"You're lucky," Guns said. "I don't think it hit anything." Then he stood a moment looking at Adam. "You made a mistake, Adam."

"Yes," Adam said.

Guns handed him the knife he had dropped as Jason came back with a cheap tin box. Guns looked through the brownish bandages and packets of folded paper. "The best thing is just let him bleed out any dirt. This won't help him."

Jason was looking at Adam. "You okay?"

"I think so," Adam said and walked over to the plane. He felt nauseous and weak, and there was pain where the bullet went in and came out, but otherwise he felt all right.

Guns went to the mouth of the revetment, picked up the dead man and brought him back to the sandbags. He slit some of the bags above him and let the sand cover him.

Adam, in pain, stood and watched him, feeling apart from Guns, and Jason and the Rebel. They knew so well what they were doing and did it so quickly and efficiently. And he, who had been told what to do, had not done it and now stood wounded, watching.

The Rebel came back into the revetment. "Don't see a thing and I don't think they heard the shot. But let's don't have any more. You don't look good with that hole in you, Adam."

"It's better than one in the head," Adam said, walking over to the plane.

The plane was sleek and apparently brand-new. He looked it over and then beckoned to the others. "See where this cable comes out," he said, pointing to the elevator control cable which came out of the fuselage through a streamlined housing and was attached to the elevator horn by a stainless steel clevis with a screw pin and lock wire. Adam untwisted the wire and unscrewed the pin. "There goes that little red wagon," he said, tossing the pin up on the revetment. "Do that to all of them."

"What does it do?" Jason asked.

"He won't have any up and down control of the tail but he won't notice it until he's going too fast to do anything about it—except run off the runway."

As they moved from plane to plane Adam knew that they were accomplishing something but, he wondered, in the end what will it amount to? The problem of getting into the Betty seemed insurmountable. And even if they got into it, how could they start the engines, wheel it around, get it to the end of the runway? It would be a long takeoff run— he figured it would take most of the runway to get the big plane off. A long run right past every gun on the island. Past the AA batteries, past the control tower with the gun slits, little black lines in the concrete, past the armed men still standing in ranks, past the tank, and artillery parked with their guns covering the runway.

It all seemed far away and totally hopeless.

And yet, Adam thought, they'd come this far and were still alive. They had come a long, long way, and a hard way, and were alive.

They gathered in the last revetment, all the planes ruined for flight, and stood, concealed, and watched the grand parade.

Adam looked at the marines, ragged and dirty and bearded, with sores oozing and the jungle rot eating away on them. They were wrecks of men and yet they were big men, and their skin—after days in the submarine and more days and nights in the wet, dark jungle—was a pale, pasty white. They were, without a doubt, United States marines.

And that was the trouble. If they had been small and yellow and almost hairless and could, as he could, speak the enemy's language they could cross the runway in full view of the parade and, perhaps, get away with it. But four big white Americans. . . .

"The problem now is to get over there," Adam said, thinking aloud. "If we weren't so white, so big and so ornery-looking . . ."

And then Adam remembered Jason capering around in the mask of the medicine man; remembered the mildewed and fusty cloaks of bird feathers. . . .

It was ridiculous. Suicidal. And yet, Adam thought, what isn't? The second those little men parading in the sun saw their faces, their eyes, they were dead. . . .

They wouldn't risk the long march across the runway. This thing must come suddenly to the enemy and surprise him and then. . . .

By the time the surprise ended they would have to be moving toward the plane. Moving fast . . .

With protection . . .

The tank.

"Jason, can you drive that tank?" Adam asked.

"I can drive anything with wheels, treads or tracks that's got an engine with spark and gas," Jason said modestly.

When Adam told them what he had in mind it made them laugh for the first time in many days. They stood in the revetment laughing, the idea appealing to them.

9 The marines and Adam crossed the runway at the seaward end—a rugged crossing, for the enemy bull-dozers had shoved the fallen tree trunks right to the sea, where they lay in a huge tangle of rotting wood constantly battered by the high, furious surf. Carrying the carved box of the native medicine men, they fought their way over the logs, one of them always on the lookout for a sentry. But for once, there were none—all, apparently, forced to parade around in the sun.

On the enemy's side of the runway at last they found a well-concealed gun position with, behind it, a bunker of logs and sandbags.

"That's one thing I don't like about 'em," Guns had said, as they crawled down into the bunker. "They're not stand-up fighters. Always shooting at you out of holes in the ground or up in the trees."

Adam remembered now the advice of one of the best class-skippers in the Pensacola Ground School. This guy could step out of ranks right in front of the officer in charge and march off—to his sack. While the rest of the platoon went to class.

"You've got to look like you just got a top-secret message from the President or, at least, the Chief of Naval Operations," this operator had explained to Adam. "If you look guilty or sneak around or run—*wham* you're in trouble. *March.* Stand up straight, chin in, gut in, butt in and march. Have the look of eagles, man, and stare straight at every officer you see. But salute real regulation. Be squared away—cap fore and aft, tie two-blocked, blouse secured. It helps to have some sort of official-looking paper in your hand, too. And don't duck around the first corner. Keep going straight away, over the horizon and away."

(This man, Adam remembered, had talent. He had flunked flight training and was a ground officer somewhere.)

They got the masks and feathers out of the chest and spread them out around the bunker. The feathers were a little ragged, chewed by the bugs, but the colors were still brilliant.

The masks were great. Made of balsa or some light wood they were hollow inside, with the features of the terrifying faces carved into the outside of the shell. To help the terror along they were painted in weird lines and spots with human hair and stiff strands of the coconut bark glued to them.

When Guns tried on one of the masks it had an odd effect on Adam. This crude mask with its daubs of paint had a curious majesty about it—a stern dignity. It diminished Guns, whose pale, infected body stood below it.

"Good," Adam said. "Now some feathers."

"And some tar and we ride him out of here on a rail," the Rebel decided.

"Look at this one!" Jason said, holding up one of the masks.

It was a fearful thing, the carved mouth pulled down in anger, the painted eyes staring and brooding, long slashes of brilliant paint ran down the cheeks, and there were gorgeous, tall feathers on the top of it.

"Vooooo-do," the Rebel said.

"This is the head man's," Jason decided.

"You wear that one, Adam," Guns said.

As they sorted out the feather cloaks Adam told them about the man who skipped classes at Pensacola. "These things are going to make us look nine feet tall anyway," he finished. "So we've got to act nine feet tall. Move real slow and dignified and stand up straight. I think we ought to keep our hands clasped like chaplains or something."

"How you going to clasp your hands with a gun in 'em?" Guns demanded.

They had not yet put on the masks but stood in the bunker looking a little ridiculous in the feathered cloaks which covered them from shoulders to ankles. Adam now looked at Guns. "I don't think we ought to take the guns," he said.

"You don't see me standing out there in this nightgown with no gun," Guns said.

"Knives perhaps," Adam said, "but no guns. What good can they do? Only harm."

Adam looked at Jason and the Rebel. Somehow Adam had a feeling that to wear these feathers and these masks and then carry guns would ruin the whole effect of the masquerade. Without guns, he thought, they could *feel* like native medicine men. With guns they'd be simply marines acting like clowns.

Guns said, "You'll never make marine, Lieutenant. A marine doesn't walk out in front of that many targets without his rifle."

The Rebel bent down, the feathers flowing, and picked up the rifle he had taken from the enemy patrol. Somehow, in contrast to the bright feathers and the awesome masks standing against the wall, the little gun looked ineffectual. It looked phony and useless. The Rebel said nothing as he put the gun back.

Jason looked at Adam. "Knives?" he asked.

"Knives okay," Adam said. "But if we've got guns and they see 'em it'll blow the whole deal."

"What do you expect us to do, walk out in front of a couple thousand soldiers like gooney birds?" Guns asked.

"Yes," Adam said. "If we do it right we can get away with it. I'll give 'em a song and dance about us natives needing some taro and yams."

Guns held the rifle out and dropped it. "So what?" he said. "We're all dead anyway."

They had to come out of the bunker to get the tall wooden masks on. Standing behind the coast-defense gun they one by one raised the masks and set them down on their shoulders. There were cords of rough bark which they tied under their arms to keep the masks in place.

When the masks were on and the feathered robes in place Adam looked at the marines and was surprised. Instead of looking (as he had feared they would) ridiculous—like scrawny clowns—they looked very tall and very dignified. Almost majestic.

"You look great!" he said. "Let's go."

When they stepped out into the sunshine the feathers shimmered and the paint of the masks picked up brighter colors.

"Ain't nobody in here but us medicine men, boss. Doodah doodah," the Rebel said. Then he swung his mask around so he could see out of the little holes in the bottom of it. For a moment he stopped walking and stood looking at Adam. "You even scare me, Adam," he said.

Adam swung around slowly so he could look down the runway. Now the parading men had stopped marching and stood at parade rest while the mechanized stuff showed off for the admiral (or whatever he was) who was now standing on a raised platform with ribbons flowing from it. There were mobile guns, caissons, armored cars, even armored motorcycles. Leading the parade was the tank, rumbling along in a cloud of dust and looking like a beribboned metal monster.

"If we could get inside that tank," Adam said, his voice muffled inside the mask, "couldn't you drive it right up beside the plane, Jason?"

"Why not?"

"Let's try it," Adam said.

Now he was walking again. Walking on the grayish coral, crushed solid by the rollers. The sun was hot, the feathers were hot, the mask awkward and chafing his shoulders. Behind him Jason, the Rebel and Guns kept pace and distance, leaving Adam walking ahead of them and alone toward the rumbling tank now coming straight toward them down the long runway.

10 The pilot of the Betty sat in the cockpit, his feet up on the instrument panel, eating little round fish balls and rice with his fingers. He was watching the parade without interest—in his job as pilot for the admiral he saw these silly parades all the time.

The pilot was only interested in saving his life. As the admiral's pilot and aide he mingled a lot with the high brass—admirals, generals, cabinet ministers, politicians—and he was convinced now that they were fools. Before he got this cushy but irritating job of flying the admiral around, he had been on Guadalcanal. He had seen the survivors from that island and he had not forgotten how absolutely whipped those men had been.

He had seen the Americans and he was afraid of them. The politicians were fools. All this, the pilot sat thinking—all the conquests in the Pacific, all the islands, *everything*—was going to be rolled up and thrown in the faces of the politicians and admirals and generals by the Americans in their mottled green uniforms that looked, to him, like dog puke. These strutting admirals in their sashes and white clothing and confidence were going to get killed. Killed by the thousands, by the millions.

The pilot was trying to figure a way not to be one of them as he sat eating and watching the parade.

They were showing off their mechanized equipment for the admiral. The tank was roaring along down the runway (and some poor pick-and-shovel laborers would have to get out here tomorrow and repair the damage the tank tracks were making in the coral of the runway—fools) with guns following.

And then, as suddenly as though they had dropped from heaven or risen, complete and tall, from the ground four native medicine men appeared walking straight toward the oncoming tank. The feathers of their cloaks were blowing in the wind, the tassels on their tall masks were streaming.

The pilot took his binoculars out of the case beside him and looked at the medicine men. Somehow the sight of them made him feel a little cold, a little afraid. The same feeling he had had as a little boy when he was taken to the temples and saw the giant idols there glaring down at him with their jeweled eyes.

The tank was bearing straight down on the four tall men but they did not change their course; they kept walking, slowly, majestically straight toward the tank. The tank was unbuttoned so the crew in the open hatch must, the pilot thought, see them. But the tank did not change course either. The corporal in charge of the tank had been given orders to drive to the end of the runway, make a 180-degree turn and come back down the other side. He had not been ordered to stop for four men dressed in masks and feathers.

11   Adam could not tell what the marines behind him were doing. He could not even tell whether they had broken and run for the shelter of the jungle or whether they were still behind him, marching with him.

Nor could he tell how far they would now go with him.

But he thought that, if they felt now as he did, they would go all the way.

Adam felt committed to this thing. As you take a monster wave and give yourself to it, knowing that it can kill you, but knowing too that you have a chance to survive it. As you take a plane into a dive-bombing attack and take it down—all the way down—so that, after you release the bomb, only your ability to fly the plane correctly will save you from going on down to collide with the sea. So far down that there's ocean spray on the bottom of the fuselage as you pull out.

He looked at the tank now looming high above him, its metal front dented from some encounter. The tracks kept coming over the top of the front rollers and going down like a metal waterfall to the surface of the runway. He could not see any sign of the waterfall or track slowing. The tank kept coming straight at him, its noise and smell now billowing over him.

Adam knew then that he, at least, had no further choice. If the marines behind him had faltered and run they still had a choice. But he did not. This tank was either going to stop or he was going to stand here and let it run over him, the hard treads of the metal tracks grinding into him and then pressing him down into the surface of the runway.

Behind Adam the three marines marched in a straight rank, abreast. Jason's mouth was dry, his tongue feeling heavy, dry and rough. His throat was dry, too. He wanted to take a deep, long, slow breath but could not.

The Rebel did not know that he was humming a song about somebody's in the kitchen with Dinah. He did not even hear his humming, as it echoed shortly around in the hollow mask standing above his head. He was looking at the blood streaming down Adam's leg.

Guns was looking through the two little holes in the mask at the long barrel of the cannon. He saw it slide over Adam's head but the mask prevented him from seeing it any longer. He could see the muzzles of the machine guns, though.

Adam stopped and the marines stopped. Adam slowly raised his arm, covered with a cloth of feathers, and held it out against the tank.

The tank stopped and the three men of the crew peered curiously down from the open hatch.

Behind this tank the guns and caissons, the armored cars —the entire column of vehicles stopped.

Adam slowly lowered his arm as the tank stood there, engine panting and gasping, hot fumes of oil sweeping from it.

The hollow mask gave Adam's voice a deep, booming, almost inhuman sound, as he called out, "Are you the chieftain of your tribe?"

The corporal of the tank shook his head. "I'm only chieftain of this tank," he said.

Without saying anything, Adam began climbing up on the tank. For a moment the crew stared at him and made involuntary movements toward the machine guns.

Adam said, "I will go with you to your chieftain."

Adam had not yet looked back but now he heard Jason say, low-voiced, "Other side."

Adam was glad that the tank crew could not see his face. He could not help grinning for now he knew that Jason, and the Rebel and Guns were still with him.

The tank began to move again with Adam and the marines on the rear deck.

The corporal asked, in childlike language, "Where you come from?"

"From the sea," Adam said.

The corporal looked at them, one by one. Jason and Guns stood with tall dignity but the Rebel said, "Doodah doodah."

Now the corporal was making his turn. The other two members of the crew stared at Adam and the marines for a moment and then faced forward.

Standing behind the crew, with the roaring of the tank's motor all around them, they could talk.

"We got to take 'em," Guns said. "Right now."

"Yeah," the Rebel said.

Adam knew that, this time, he should use the knife correctly. That he would, finally, *have* to use it.

But the action must be hidden from the drivers of the vehicles behind the tank. Someone must prevent them from seeing the movement.

Jason said, "Adam, spread those feathers out so nobody can see."

In the masks it was hard to see anything except what was directly in front of you. Adam spread his arms out, the feathered cloak falling from them and flowing in the wind.

He hoped it would be enough as Jason, Guns and the Rebel moved toward the open hatch.

One of the crew must have sensed that they were coming for he turned and when he saw the knives he screamed. But it didn't do any good.

"Get this thing off me," Jason said.

"Hold these guys up!" Guns said. "Keep us covered, Adam."

Adam stood with his arms outstretched, the feathers blowing.

The Rebel got the mask off Jason and he slid down through the hatch, still in the feathers.

"Move up slow, Adam," the Rebel said.

Adam moved up to the hatch.

"Hold him," Guns said.

Adam took the corporal under the arms and held him upright in the open hatch. Guns and the Rebel each held a dead man up, the pretty ribbons streaming from the football helmets.

Down inside the tank Jason was sitting in a tractor seat with long levers on each side of it. As he worked these levers, and the bare metal foot pedals, he looked up toward them. "What do I do now?" he asked.

Adam turned his shoulders slowly, moving the mask so that he could see out of the little peepholes.

Behind the tank the other vehicles followed steadily, in line, equally spaced down the runway. Directly behind the tank there was a long cannon of some sort being drawn by a small tractor. The driver had a scarf wrapped around his nose and mouth to keep out the billows of grayish coral dust blowing back on him from the tank's tracks, but his eyes, Adam could see, were looking at him with interest.

"Those guys behind us can see everything we do," Adam told the Rebel.

The tank, with its steel tracks biting into the coral of the runway, created more dust than the other vehicles, but each one of them, in turn, moved through the dust cloud of the ones in front and added its own cloud to the big one.

The tank was moving straight into the steady wind which, Adam estimated, was blowing at about ten knots.

"How fast are we going?" he called down to Jason.

"This thing reads in kilometers," Jason called up. "Twenty kilometers, it says."

Six times twenty divided by ten. Twelve miles an hour. "Slow it down to fifteen kilometers," Adam told him," and as soon as the rest slow down, we'll make a hundred-and-eighty turn and go back toward the plane."

He heard the diesel slowing and turned his mask again to look back. For a few minutes the change of speed upset the timing of the column behind but at last they adjusted. "Okay, turn her," Adam said.

Jason swung the tank in a wide turn, the other vehicles following in his tracks on the coral, and headed back down the runway.

Adam watched the dust at the end of the column and called down to Jason, "Still too fast, Jason. Slow to ten kilometers."

Again the change of speed made the vehicles behind bunch up for a moment, then they began to string out again —and disappear. The cloud of dust they created was caught and lifted by the wind and blown back over them.

It evidently infuriated the drivers. As the dust cloud billowed over them Adam could see them making wild motions at the tank to speed up.

Jason held it at ten kilometers.

The dust sifting into the masks was gritty with a faint, faint fishy smell. Looking back Adam could barely make out the shape of the tractor following behind, and barely see the still furious arm waving of the driver.

"How close can you get to the wing of the plane?" Adam called down to Jason.

"How many coats of paint you want scraped off?"

"Come as close as you can." Adam turned to the Rebel. "I want to get this mask and stuff off. We'll put it on this one." He touched one of the dead crew. "Then when we pass the plane I'll try to get up on the wing. In the dust they may not see me."

"By yourself?"

"Jason will swing the tank around behind the plane. Then you all come over. Wear the masks. Say 'doodah doodah' if they stop you. Try to make it fast before the dust settles. But walk. Don't run."

"I'll be too scared to run."

Adam looked at the wooden, impassive face staring with its painted wooden eyes. "You don't look scared," he said.

The tank made a tremendous amount of noise, the diesel roaring, the tracks clanking around and around, the rollers squeaking.

Adam looked ahead. The band, in its white uniforms, was playing away—he could see the drummer banging, see the trombone slides moving in and out—but he could hear nothing over the noise of the tank.

As a particularly big cloud of dust swept toward him he stooped and said, "Okay, help me off with this thing."

The Rebel got the mask off and down on the shoulders of the dead man as Adam got down into the hatch of the tank and stripped off the feathers. He noticed now that he was bleeding from both the bullet holes and the sight of the blood seemed to allow him to notice the sharp pain in his body.

Adam crouched in the hatch as he looked ahead at the plane. It sat there so still, so lifeless and pretty, the silver propellers unmoving, the long tapered wings rocking a little in the wind . . .

In the plane the pilot was annoyed with the admiral, who insisted that, whenever there was a parade, the pilot wear full uniform complete with sash and side arms. The pistol belt was hot around his waist, the pistol and ammunition a heavy, useless weight.

But the parade would soon be over, he hoped. The silly tank was about to pass in review. Then the admiral would tell the commanding officer what was wrong with his outfit, get in the plane and fly away.

The pilot looked out the wide window at the approaching tank, moving with only its nose really clear of the cloud of dust. The wild-looking medicine men were still aboard it, those feathers and painted masks showing through the dust.

He thought there had been four of them. Now he could only see two. Possibly the other two were down in the tank selling souvenirs of the South Seas to the tank crewmen. . . .

The parade would soon be over. The pilot started to unbuckle the pistol belt, then changed his mind. The admiral was an observant, fat little fool. He'd notice a thing like that.

The pilot settled back into his seat to wait, the roar of the approaching column of vehicles and the noise of the band drowning out the broadcast he had been listening to on the plane's radio.

12 "You won't even have to jump for it," Jason told Adam. "I'll go under the wing so you can just step off."

Adam didn't say anything. His throat was too dry as he crouched, almost naked, in the hatch, his blood running down his flanks and dripping on the hot metal platform.

He waited, gauging his distance as well as he could through the dust, as the tank moved on toward the long, graceful wing.

Now he could see the stall-out ribbons moving a little in the wind, see the aileron hinges, prettily faired into the wing. He looked up at the Rebel standing up there nine feet tall in the mask. "As soon as you all get in the plane, Reb, close and lock the door because we're going to take off like that great stripy bird."

"That's what Ah lak about the South."

The wing was over the front of the tank now. Adam came out of the hatch, put both hands on the moving wing and easily got up on it. As the tank passed from under him he began to run along the wing, being careful to step on top of the ribs with his bare and now bloody feet which left footprints along the wing.

The tank rumbled on and then, with one track locked, Jason spun it around so that the long, thin-barreled cannon pointed toward the troops in ranks; pointed over the heads of the men of the band playing away.

Guns, awkward in his mask and feathers, was still studying the heavy Nambu machine gun mounted behind a little barrier of steel plate. He had already figured out the cannon.

The dust was still all around them and, as an afterthought, Jason had turned the selector up to full rich and left the tank's engine running so that it was now pouring out gouts of black exhaust.

The Rebel was helping Jason get the mask back on (they left Adam's mask over the head of the dead crewman).

The rest of the parade of vehicles went streaming past the halted tank, their dust flowing into the black of the exhaust.

The tank motor roared at half-throttle, the engines of the other vehicles roared out of the cloud of dust, the band played.

No one heard the shot except Adam. . . .

The pilot thought at first that it was the tank passing by, but as the tank went on and then slewed around and stopped, but the plane kept shaking, he wondered what else could be making it shake that way.

The pilot looked out the side window and saw a tall, half-naked Caucasian running carefully along the wing. The man was bleeding from a wound in the side; he seemed to have infected sores on his arms and legs; he had not shaved and looked, to the pilot, insane.

The pilot got the pistol out of its holster and aimed it at the running man, resting his arm on the edge of the cockpit window. He aimed well and fired.

The impact of the bullet spun the Caucasian around in a weird, awkward dance and the pilot thought that he fell as a cloud of dust swept up over the wing and obscured everything for a moment.

Then, when the dust cleared, the man was no longer on the wing and the pilot decided that the shot had killed him and he had fallen and rolled off the wing. The pilot got up out of the seat, ducked low in the cramped cockpit, and went aft so that he could look out the window and under the wing.

13 Adam never even saw the pilot aiming the gun out of the cockpit window. He was running along the wing, watching for the little lines of the wing ribs and at the same time watching Jason wheel the tank around and stop it. Everything was going fine. There would be the dust of the other vehicles to conceal them and now black smoke was pouring out of the tank.

Adam thought, now for the first time, that they really had a chance to get into the plane—all of them.

And then something hit him. It struck him as solidly as a swinging baseball bat or a speeding car would strike. He felt himself being spun completely around by whatever hit him. But then he was facing toward the open side door of the plane again. Through the dust and the sudden dimness of his eyes he could only see it as a dark, rectangular place in the gray, darkening air. He went toward it without knowing that he was now down on his hands and knees, a great flow of blood staining the silver wing.

Thought; the recognition of things; feeling; the sense of time and distance—all of these were fading out of Adam. Now he was face down, pulling himself along with his hands, pushing himself with knees growing steadily weaker. He did not feel the dark coolness of the inside of the plane but that was as far as he could go. He stopped there in the aisle of the plane. His last thought was that he should rest a moment now. Rest, and then go on.

BOOK FOUR
The Valley of the Shadow of Death

1   Adam Land, wounded to the point of death, was awakened by a sound. The sound, being different and closer than the other sounds around him, struck through to the mechanism of his brain, as yet unwounded, and woke him up.

He found that he was slumped, half sitting, with his back against some metal object. His bare and boody legs and feet stretched out awkwardly down what appeared to be a narrow corridor. Blood was pouring from some wound in his body and there were flies around him.

There was light coming from somewhere, but the place was fairly dark and cool.

Perhaps, he thought, he was in some sort of church, for there were pews, thickly padded, on each side of the aisle he lay in.

There was a window and through it he could see the tops of green palm trees, the fronds waving to him in the wind.

He was in a church. Or perhaps lying in the aisle of an airplane.

An odd thought, like a complete little cloud drifting in an empty sky, floated into and across and out of his mind. He thought: I am the only American left alive on this island. Something has happened to all the rest and I am the only American left alive anywhere in the world. If this is true, he thought, then I am the only person who knows what it feels like to be an American. The only person who knows *how* to be an American.

Then he said to himself, "I'd better not die. Not because I'm important, but because what I know is important. No, I'd better not die."

Then that thought drifted away and he wondered again what had waked him up. There was music coming from somewhere but that had not waked him. It seemed to him that it had been a voice. A voice close to him and, now remembering it, full of menace.

Adam looked then at the details of his situation. He was hurt for blood was coming out of him and the flies were buzzing around, lighting and flying again. Purposeless, they seemed. But there had been purpose in the voice which had awakened him; purpose and threat.

There were some shoes near him. Shoes with high uppers; shoes such as they wore in Texas and the Air Corps—boots almost.

White trousers were above the shoes and above the trousers was a white jacket with a pretty red sash across it.

Adam raised his head a little higher. The pilot was standing there looking down at him, a pistol in his hand.

To Adam the pilot looked small and—mean. He would have preferred an enemy of great height and strength and, even with the gift of death, dignity. Not this little meanness like a bad-tempered little feisty dog.

It wasn't really the enemy in his white clothes and pretty sash.

It was the pistol.

Even the pistol was of no stature and it was shoddily made and badly put together, the parts of it not fitting properly, the trigger guard screwed on and the screw slots burred by carelessness. There were even rusty spots on the enemy's pistol and Adam doubted if the action worked with the creamy smoothness of a marine's gun.

It was not good, Adam thought. The enemy was small and mean and his pistol was mean and rusty and, the marines said, made a disagreeable, angry little yelp when it fired. It had none of the power and authority of a Colt .45, none of that arm-jarring slam of the .45.

But it could kill you, this little gun. And it was going to kill him.

Adam remembered now what had awakened him. It had been the enemy saying, in English, "American, you die."

Adam could do nothing. His wounds held him with simple weakness against the seat, all of his strength having drained out of him. He could not raise his hand, nor draw up his legs to rise from the floor. It took all his strength just to raise his head high enough so that he could look beyond the pistol to the face of the enemy.

Above the immediate silence between him and the enemy Adam heard the band playing, the tank motor running, even the pounding of the surf. But no voice.

It was not right.

Adam looked at his enemy and said in the enemy's own oddly soft and singsong language; said it aloud and with authority. "I will not die in this contemptible fashion!"

So he tried to rise to his feet but was struck down again.

Adam heard the explosion of the gun so close to his head

that it added a small, sharp hurt to all the pain. Then a slow darkness moved toward him, covered him, pressed him completely down into his own blood on the floor.

2   "Is Adam dead?" Jason asked as he and the Rebel rolled the dead pilot off of Adam. They were still wearing the masks and feathers as they pulled Adam up off the floor and got him into one of the plane's seats.

"I think so," the Rebel said, pulling his mask off and throwing it away.

"No, he's breathing. Adam! Adam!"

Guns was climbing into the plane now, the mask striking against the doorframe and falling back out of the plane.

"Lock the door!" the Rebel said to Guns. "Then see if there're any guns. Adam's hit bad."

"Help me," Adam said and tried to point, his hand feeble as it waved toward the cockpit.

Jason and the Rebel got him under the arms and knees and carried him forward through the plane. They hurt him getting him into the pilot's seat, but he did not feel it. Jason got into the copilot's seat and leaned over to Adam. "Tell me what to do, Adam!"

The cockpit was spinning slowly around, spinning and spinning. But then, gradually, it stopped going all the way around and just rocked gently from side to side.

"Mixture . . ." Adam said, his voice trailing off to nothing, then coming back, ". . . rich . . ."

"Where is it? *Where*, Adam? *Where?*"

Jason's voice sounded far away to him as he sat staring at the instruments which continued to rock slowly back and forth.

"Can he see?" the Rebel asked, standing behind the seats. "Can he think?"

Adam looked at the graceful little symbols, little red and black symbols which, to him, looked as though drawn on the instrument panel by a child. A nice, orderly child, Adam thought.

He found the symbol for the mixture setting and tried to push it. Jason put his hand on top of Adam's and together they pushed the control forward.

"Props . . . full r.p.m." Adam looked and found the symbol and Jason pushed the two levers to the stops.

"Unlock controls," Adam said, pointing to the lock.

"Roll out controls."

"Unlock instruments."

"The flaps . . ." Adam said, trying to lean over so that he could see the handles.

"This it?" Jason asked.

"No. That's throttle. There . . . over there."

"All the way?"

"All the way," Adam said. "Now that," he said, pointing. "Turn it. And hold it . . . No, wait! Put your feet on those pedals. Push hard. Now turn."

Outside, the port propeller quivered, jerked, stopped, jerked again, revolved once, stopped, revolved again and then suddenly, with a gush of flame and smoke, began to spin.

"Cowl flaps . . . where?" Adam asked, studying the symbols. "There . . . stream cowl flaps. Is everybody in?"

"Everybody in. Can you fly it, Adam?"

"Now turn that one. Push on the pedals."

Both propellers spun now.

Trim tabs, Adam thought. Where are the trim tabs? He couldn't find them. No, there they were, in the wrong place.

Now Adam put his bloody hand on the throttles and tried to push them forward but his hand, slippery with blood, would not stay on the red knobs of the throttles. Again Jason put his hand on top of Adam's. "Stay with it, Adam," Jason said. "You're going real good. Stay with it."

"Can we go?" the Rebel asked. "They're coming."

"We can go," Adam said.

3 When Guns had climbed into the plane and had seen Adam he remembered other men he had seen as seriously wounded. He remembered the effect of such massive wounds. Some men, so hit, could not function at all and died. Others, of, Guns always thought, sterner caliber could function, but not for long, and they could not sustain it. For a moment they would be capable of clear and rational thought, then as though engulfed in the pain of the wound, they would drift out of the world and be no good for the purpose at hand.

Adam was terribly wounded. If he could function at all it would be a miracle. If he could not, Guns had decided, then the plane was no place for him, Guns.

Guns had decided to go back to the tank. If Adam could get the plane started there would be time for Guns to get back aboard. In the tank he could, perhaps, give Adam the extra time he would need.

As Jason and the Rebel picked Adam up and started toward the cockpit with him, Guns backed out of the plane's door, closed it and locked it.

Guns had knocked off the mask he had been wearing as he got into the plane and now it was lying on the ground, the grim face of the mask facing up.

It had an odd effect on Guns. He stopped for a moment to look at it and then to look down at himself, the cloak of feathers concealing his U.S. marine fatigues.

Guns kicked the mask away and ripped off the feathers. Then he felt again that he was a marine.

He ran, keeping close to the plane, ducking under the tail of it and then ran on, stooped low, toward the tank. He went up the side of it still on the run, his bare feet stepping from the warm coral runway to the roller pin, to the track guard, to the deck, to the edge of the hatch. Then he was down inside the tank whose engine was still roaring, making everything rattle.

Guns looked out of the machine-gun slit, studying his field of fire.

The plane was parked, headed into the wind, on the side of the runway and about halfway down the length of it. Between the tail of the plane and the concrete control tower Guns squatted beside the machine gun in the tank. The rest of the vehicles had gone on and were now drawn up in front of the parading troops.

Guns looked over at the plane. The propellers were not moving, there was no sound from it.

The tank was facing the troops and Guns could see now that the officers were beginning to suspect something. They were running around, shouting and pointing, or were gathered in groups staring at the tank and the plane and arguing.

The band dribbled to a stop.

His field of fire was from the corner of the control tower to the plane's elevator. Guns was satisfied with it.

He checked the machine gun and threaded the belted ammo into it, hand-cranking a round into the chamber and leaving the gun ready. Then he studied the aiming mechanism of the long cannon sticking out of the tank's turret and now pointing straight at the men of the band. He would use the cannon only if the situation got organized and they unlimbered some of the artillery which was now still hooked to the tractors and caissons. The machine gun would have to do all the work, Guns decided—if any work had to be done.

There was still no sound, no movement from the plane. He

doubted now if Adam was still alive. He had had the gray look of death when Guns had looked at him and death was not far away.

But, Guns decided, he would not start this thing. He looked at the men in their white uniforms. Let them start it, he decided.

He wished that the Rebel and Jason would get out of the plane and get over here in the tank. They'd come in handy when the scuffle started. Jason on the cannon, the Rebel on the other machine gun, and him on this one. The three of them would be hard to handle—for a little while.

Guns could tell now that some officer over there was making a decision and, sure enough, some of the troops got their rifle butts up off the ground and started loading them.

Now, with about a dozen soldiers walking in front, a little group of officers followed and the whole detail started toward the plane.

Behind this little group the rest of the troops began to mill around; nobody knowing what to do.

Guns knew exactly what to do. He checked the ammo belt to see that it was feeding straight into the gun and was lying in nice, even folds in the cans.

Then he bent down over the gun and looked along it to the right sight. First he got the ring sight in good focus and then let it blur as he brought the walking group up sharp. He still had a little time before they would be in a position where he could rake them with the shortest burst so he looked over at the troops, searching among them until he found the little guy he had seen get out of the plane. Guns didn't know what he was—admiral, general—but he'd been taught that the best way to mess up a bunch of troops was to get rid of the officers, starting, if you could, with the top brass and working down.

It wasn't going to be hard, Guns decided. The officers all wore those fancy sashes. Imagine!

Now the party advancing on the plane was close to it and the riflemen were beginning to deploy, getting ready to give the brave officers some cover as they moved on to the plane.

Poor Jason and the Rebel would be caught in there like rats.

Guns let the people blur again and started the slow squeeze, his other hand on the gun in case it wanted to climb, his shoulder and chest jammed up hard against the curved butt of the thing.

This machine gun didn't have the satisfying crash of the big .50's in the marine corps tanks, but, Guns had to admit, it had a higher rate of fire. He was wasting ammo at this high rate, so he got off the trigger.

The empty brass was bouncing all over the tank as he swung the gun fast around and got the admiral or general or whatever he was in the sight and let go with one round.

It was a good, accurate gun. Guns saw the admiral or general go down, so then he sprayed the group around him with a short burst before swinging the gun back to cover the approach to the plane.

Guns was surprised to see one of the plane's propellers begin to turn over.

Adam must be alive, he thought. The Rebel and Jason weren't smart enough to figure out an airplane, much less this one. He had to admire Adam. Hit like that it was hard to think, hard to get things done. But now the other prop was spinning.

And the fun was over. Guns had panicked them for a little while but now they were breaking for cover; stuff was hitting the tank, making him feel as though he were inside a big tin drum. He spotted three of them down on the ground setting up a tripod with a light machine gun on top of it.

He wiped that and then gave the whole outfit a hosing. This put them down for a moment, so, just in case, he cranked the cannon around and up and sent a round through the glass window of the control tower.

About ten guys were frantically trying to swing one of the artillery guns around and get it set so he took care of them and hosed the whole outfit down again, watching the belt uncoiling from the ammo box and looking around for more belts.

The smart boys were getting back into the trees and behind the buildings. More and more stuff was hitting the tank and the plane's props were blowing clouds of dust over it making it hard for Guns to pick his targets.

"Get that thing out of here," Guns said, angrily, glaring at the plane he could barely see through the dust.

The Guns' anger died and he was sad because, now, he would never be able to tell Adam that he was as good a marine as Guns had ever served with. A marine.

"There's a war going on," the Rebel said.

4   Adam was having trouble now with things moving in and out of focus as he searched the panel for the fuel selector. Later, he told himself. "Let's go," he said.

"Can you make it?" Jason asked.

"Yeah," Adam said and was surprised that he knew now that he could. He got one hand on the throttle knobs and the other around the yoke. "Keep your feet hard on those pedals," he told Jason. "The great stripy bird."

"They're all goofed up," the Rebel said, looking out the window. "They're shooting up their own tank."

Adam pushed the throttles forward as fast as the engines could take it. The waves that were rolling through his brain were coming faster now and each one seemed to black him out for a longer time. He knew he couldn't last to check the magnetos but the engines were going smoothly. He held the yoke forward to keep the plane from leaping off the ground when Jason let go on the brakes.

"Off the pedals!" Adam said.

The plane seemed to jump forward, then it slowed a little and began to roll.

Adam could feel, in the back of his head, a wave of the sick darkness rolling toward him. He held it back and looked out at the shortening runway streaming under the nose of the plane. He would let it roll all the way. Let it roll to the lagoon. . . .

He looked for and found the landing-gear control and showed it to Jason. He wanted those wheels to start up the instant they left the ground—if they ever did. But not before. Not a second too soon or the plane would go down on its belly; nor too late, adding drag that could pull them into the lagoon. "I'll say 'Up!'" he told Jason.

He was running out of runway, the blue water of the lagoon seeming to come at him too fast. Then he had to translate kilometers per hour into knots to figure his ground speed. Six tenths . . .

Guns, in the tank, kept the enemy down with short bursts from the machine gun, between bursts watching the plane as it lumbered down the runway. It seemed to him to be going too slow ever to lift itself off the ground and he felt sorry for Adam and Jason and the Rebel. It had been a good try—a pity it had to end with the plane in the lagoon.

Guns felt a tingle of fear as he saw the wheels of the plane folding backward. Now, he thought, the plane was going to drop down on its silver belly and crash right at the end of the runway. He had seen planes do this and had wondered how the enormous fire could start so instantly.

The wheels kept folding and the plane went neither up nor

down. It passed over the end of the coral runway and was out over the lagoon now.

Guns laughed aloud in the tank. If there had been waves in that lagoon; waves only a foot high, the plane would never have cleared them. It was the best piece of flying he had ever seen and he said, in a whisper, "Go go go!"

Guns saw some of the troops appearing again and he swung the gun on them. It fired a dozen times and then stopped firing in mid-burst.

It did not surprise Guns, for he had been expecting it and knew that the ammo belt had been exhausted.

But the plane was slowly pulling itself up and he still had the cannon, the barbette moved by the still running engine of the tank.

Guns settled down now to take care of the enemy's anti-aircraft guns. He picked out the long sky-pointing barrels of them and shot at their bases with the cannon, the tank jerking back on its treads at every round.

He shot all the ammo for the cannon and then looked around in the tank for some small-arms stuff. They were, he decided, going to have to get him out of this tank with a can opener.

The plane was now just a pencil line in the sky, two dots in the line.

Guns aimed the small-caliber rifle carefully at a group of the enemy cranking up a flame thrower. . . .

The Rebel, who had been standing in the narrow space just behind the two pilot's seats turned back into the plane and said, "How about that, Guns. We all is flyin' lak . . ." Then he stopped talking and walked slowly back into the plane. He walked all the way back to the head and pulled aside the curtain. "Guns?" he said. "Guns?"

The Rebel turned and went back to the cockpit. He leaned

down so he could see Adam's face. Under the dirty beard Adam's skin was gray and his clenched teeth made the muscles stand out.

The Rebel leaned down close to Jason, "Guns isn't here," he told him.

Jason swung around. "You're nuts!"

"No. I think he went back to the tank."

"What *for?*" Jason yelled.

"There was a real war going on when we took off. Between them and the tank. Guns."

Jason looked at the Rebel for a moment, his mouth set hard to keep anything from showing. Then he said, "Guns'll give 'em hell."

"He sho' will," the Rebel said.

Adam said, "In case I can't manage it, here's what you do, Jason."

It took him a long time to show Jason. He kept forgetting things, leaving out things but at last he showed Jason how to hold it steady on the course he hoped would take them near the American-held island of Samoa. To fly straight and level. Then Adam said, "I'm going to sleep a little while."

Jason held the yoke with tense hands, his eyes straining between the airspeed meter and the altimeter. The Rebel leaned down close to him and said, "Is he going to wake up, Jason?"

"See what you can do for him," Jason said. "I'm flying."

All the Rebel could do for Adam was to slow the draining away of his blood. When he finished Jason asked, "How bad is it?"

"Anybody else would be dead." Then he looked at Jason. "How are we going to get down from here, Jason?"

Jason allowed his eyes to leave the instruments long enough to look over at Adam. Adam looked dead as he lay slumped in the seat, the bloody seat belt holding the Rebel's bandaging in place. Then Jason looked at the Rebel. "He'll get us down, Reb."

5   For four hours Adam sat in the pilot's seat held upright by the belt and shoulder harness, his head lying to one side, his eyes closed. Many times during the hours the Rebel and Jason thought that he had, finally, died, but he did not die. He gave no sign of consciousness, said nothing, apparently did not hear anything they said.

But, after four hours, he suddenly opened his eyes and said, "How long, Jason?"

"Four hours and ten minutes."

"See anything?"

"Water."

"We'll radio Samoa," Adam said and then, as though he were perfectly healthy, he told Jason how to turn on and tune the radio, reading the little, strange symbols. The Rebel hung the microphone around Adam's neck and then held the push-to-talk button for Adam didn't have strength enough.

Adam called in the clear, asking for Radio Samoa and even managed to smile a little as Samoa answered almost at once.

"This is Lieutenant Adam Land, Naval Reserve. I'm flying a captured enemy twin-engined Betty at angels 10 on course 187, speed 180. Request course to Samoa field. Over."

The flat voice of Radio Samoa said, "Bogey at angels 10, course 187, speed 180. It's a Betty. Go get him!"

"No!" Adam tried to shout into the microphone. "Leave us alone, please! This is not a trick. We are unarmed, without bombs. There are only me and three marines. United States marines. My number is 070562—look it up. Land, Adam Land."

"Planes!" the Rebel said, pointing out the side window. There were six Navy F2F's speeding down on them.

Adam said nothing and when the Rebel looked at him his head had fallen over again, his eyes closed again.

The Rebel got the microphone off of Adam and held it in his hand. "Listen heah, you all," he said into the mike. "You shoot down this heah plane and Ah'm comin' back to ha'nt you. You navy swab handles, *you*. We done brought this plane from way out yonder and we want to land it. We got a wounded navy pilot aboard."

The flat voice of Radio Samoa came in then, "You are cleared to land, Betty. But if you open your bomb bay or man your guns we will shoot you down. Acknowledge."

"Okay," the Rebel said and looked again at Adam. "Listen, down there," he said into the mike. "We may not be able to get this plane down in one piece. So take this down. Write it down. We are Operation Moondance. We've come from Island Moondance and here's what's on it. Write this down because that's what we went out there to find out. They've got eighteen coast-defense guns on concrete pads that can cover any landing, sea or lagoon. They've got thirty-six anti-aircraft guns, Nambu or Bofors. Troops estimated at two thousand and apparently well trained . . ." The Rebel went on, reeling off the details of the defense on Moondance.

When he stopped Adam suddenly said, "And that tank, Reb."

The Rebel had purposely left out the tank because, with Guns in it, there wouldn't be much left of the tank by the time they got Guns out of it.

Or much left of Guns, the Rebel thought, and wondered why it was always the best guys who got it.

"There's the island," Jason said. "Can you see it, Adam?"

Adam strained to sit up and the Rebel helped him.

Below them Samoa was green and beautiful and peaceful with the long landing strip cut, as on Moondance, through the groves of coconut palms. They could see the neat little houses of the native communities, see the churches and schoolhouses.

"I've got it," Adam said, lifting his hands to the yoke.

Beside them the Navy F2F's flew in formation, ready to shoot if a gun on the Betty moved, or the bomb bays as much as cracked open.

The Betty swung into its approach and settled toward the earth. "Gear down," Adam said. "Flaps down."

Jason looked at him. He was sitting almost erect, his head up, his eyes moving from the instruments to the field ahead of them.

Now the runway was streaming under them. Then the wheels touched with a little scream of rubber. Adam reversed pitch of the props and cut the throttles.

As the engine stopped and the plane stopped rolling it seemed to Jason and the Rebel strangely quiet and suddenly hot inside the plane.

Outside, a jeep, loaded with officers, came tearing down the runway. And off to the left Jason saw machine guns concealed in the low undergrowth.

"Don't take a deep breath, Reb," Jason whispered. "There're marines behind those guns."

They heard the jeep roar up and stop outside. Then a voice yelled, "Open up and come out with your hands up."

Jason leaned out the window. "We got a wounded officer in here, sir. Wounded bad."

"All right, we're coming in. Remember, no tricks. You're covered."

"Tricks!" the Rebel said to nobody, going aft to open the door.

The officers, armed with carbines and looking as though

they were about to use them, came cautiously into the plane. But when they saw the Rebel they relaxed a little.

The Rebel followed them respectfully as they marched forward through the plane to the cockpit. "Who's the pilot?" an officer asked.

Jason pointed at Adam who had slumped back into the seat. His head was hanging down on his chest now. Jason had not noticed that and he gently raised Adam's head and let it rest on the back of the seat.

For a moment it did not seem important but then, slowly, Jason put out his hand again and touched Adam on the throat.

So cold, so cold and still. "He's dead," Jason said.

"Who is he?" the officer asked.

Jason looked up at him. Jason's throat was so tight it hurt and suddenly his head ached behind his eyes.

Jason said to the officer, "A marine."

About the Author

Robb White has actually lived the adventurous life that most people only dream of. He was born in the Philippine Islands, where his father was a missionary, never went to school (there weren't any) until he attended the Episcopal High School in Alexandria, Virginia, and from there entered the Naval Academy at Annapolis. All the while he was determined to be a writer; he resigned his commission, held various jobs and finally sold a story to the *American Boy*. After this success he went back to sea, serving on an assortment of vessels, and in his wanderings managed to write several novels. During World War II he served in the Navy with the Pacific fleet. Now a captain in the Naval Reserve, Robb White lives in Malibu, California, where he spends most of his time writing books, movies and television scripts.